SF Grimoire
Grimoire anthology. V
IV, Royal will

GRIMOIRE
ANTHOLOGY

VOLUME IV
THE ROYAL WILL

Destiny Universe Created by Bungie

To our community,
You've become the main characters in the stories we tell.
You've filled our worlds with your light and your friendship.
Thank you for your passion for our games and for each other.
Most of all, thank you for playing.

foreword

Everything is a team effort when you make a video game like *Destiny*.

Story, especially.

In a novel, the author has absolute control over the universe they conjure. They are at leisure to curate their world, characters, and plot as they prefer. They can draft, then reflect, and then draft again.

Filmmakers take time to reflect, too—it is said that many great films were only found in the edit.

Writing story for a video game, you must reflect as you create, not afterward. Everyone on the project is an author. Control is shared among the team. Narrative experts shepherd the story as the whole team pitches, collaborates, constrains, and negotiates together to find resonant ideas. Key elements are continually added, removed, or reimagined.

At Bungie, we often talk about "strong ideas, loosely held" because we must always be receptive to change when we pursue excellence. We seek chemistry when brainstorming and clarity when communicating. When we must pivot, we try to remain graceful and good-humored. Through all this hard work, every day brings humbling new evidence that our peers are both talented and passionate.

I learned the strength of these principles during the development of *Destiny 2: Forsaken*. We thought hard about how to reignite the story of *Destiny: The Taken King* in a way that would be both satisfying for veterans and approachable for newcomers. We brainstormed, debated, playtested. (Another Bungie principle: "show early, show often.") We reflected often on our central narrative theme: *the thin line between Light and Dark*.

We had rich metaphors to aid our exploration: Taken corruption as a symbol of poison, possession, and delirium; Drifter's audacious Gambit and Ahamkara wishes as casual shortcuts to seductive powers; the orderly operations of the Tower and the lawless frontier of the Tangled Shore; the pristine overworld of the Dreaming City and its hellish underbelly; the transformative power of tricks and secrets.

The Awoken, too, are born from Light and Dark—selflessness and selfishness, good intentions and guarded truths. They live in the Reef on humanity's outer edge, the only significant post-Collapse colony located between Sol and the heliopause beyond. Despite that tension, the Awoken represent humanity's hopeful will to overcome against long odds: *"I see our path ahead,"* Sjur Eido says, *"full of despair and hardship, and I will walk it with joy in my heart."*

Given the chance to live in utopia, the Awoken chose instead to stand in defense of humanity. When you think of them, remember Mara Sov and the fleet that broke against Oryx's Dreadnaught. Remember Uldren Sov and Jolyon Till, forever changed by the Black Garden. Remember the vigilkeepers in the Dreaming City—Petra Venj, Amrita Vae, the Corsairs, the Techeuns. Cursebreakers, Chroniclers, remember the legend of Sjur Eido. Most of all, remember the Guardians who protect the Last City—Commander Zavala, Asher Mir, Tyra Karn, Crow, and perhaps even you, cousin.

Look for the Light in these stories. Now more than ever, hope is a discipline. Practice it wherever you go.

Mallory "Z" Schleif
2021

introduction

All fictional worlds are, at their core, a conversation: between characters, between creators and fans, between the teams of creators who build and nurture them.

As creators, our conversations for the *War Machines* volume began with a hope that it would be the only *Destiny Grimoire Anthology* crafted in the midst of a global pandemic. That hope did not come true. We have all endured an extraordinary year and more. We have been asked to show up for one another in unprecedented ways.

And when we found ourselves tired, sad, isolated, depleted—we sought refuge and sustenance in fictional worlds. If *Destiny* has been that for you, even for a single hour, please know that being there for you was, and always is, an honor.

Now, let's throw ourselves into a discussion about fictional worlds for a bit, shall we?

I have always thought of *Destiny* as a science-fantasy story: lasers and legends, advanced technology and incomprehensible powers. Fantastical past and uncertain future.

Nowhere is this more true than with the Awoken. They are a fantasy: elfin, monarchical, long-lived. And they reflect the questions sci-fi writers have been asking for decades: What is the next step in human evolution? What will humanity become?

Many of you choose to play as Awoken, adopting the role of beings who were twice-alienated: both by the amnesia of a Guardian's resurrection and the trauma of an undesired transformation. What was it about the Awoken that drew you to them? Did you like the idea of being a mystery to your own self? Both human and alien—both "us" and "other"? Perhaps even identify with them a bit?

We've all fought for the Awoken, wielding Light to protect both the Earthbound Awoken and their cousins in the distant Reef. The Reef Awoken didn't trust you. Not at first. But your pursuit of knowledge proved you worthy of it; you were inducted into Queen Mara's confidence. And you became a part of the story of the Awoken, only a small fraction of which is recounted in the pages of this book.

Those who walk in the Traveler's Light are forever changed and are a part of the conversation that is *Destiny*. And the Awoken, with their deep history, their uncanny technology, their loyalty and strategy and hope, are both inhuman and fantastically, inevitably human.

Jill Scharr
2021

Prologue

I drive myself to the edge of madness trying to explain the truth.

It's so simple. Elegant like a knife point. It explains - this is not hyperbole, this is the farthest thing from exaggeration - EVERYTHING.

But you lay it out and they stare at you like you've just been exhaling dust. Maybe they're missing some underlying scaffold of truth. Maybe they are all propped on a bed of lies that must be burned away.

Why does anything exist?

No no no no no don't reach for that word. There's no 'reason'. That's teleology and teleology will stitch your eyelids shut.

Why do we have atoms? Because atomic matter is more stable than the primordial broth. Atoms defeated the broth. That was the first war. There were two ways to be and one of them won. And everything that came next was made of atoms.

Atoms made stars. Stars made galaxies. Worlds simmered down to rock and acid and in those smoking primal seas the first living molecule learned to copy itself. All of this happened by the one law, the blind law, which exists without mind or meaning. It's the simplest law but it has no worshippers here (out there, though, out there - !)

HOW DO I EXPLAIN IT it's so simple WHY DON'T YOU SEE

Imagine three great nations under three great queens. The first queen writes a great book of law and her rule is just. The second queen builds a high tower and her people climb it to see the stars. The third queen raises an army and conquers everything.

The future belongs to one of these queens. Her rule is harshest and her people are unhappy. But she rules.

This explains everything, understand? This is why the universe is the way it is, and not some other way. Existence is a game that everything plays, and some strategies are winners: the ability to exist, to shape existence, to remake it so that your descendants - molecules or stars or people or ideas - will flourish, and others will find no ground to grow.

And as the universe ticks on towards the close, the great players will face each other. In the next round there will be three queens and all of them will have armies, and now it will be a battle of swords - until one discovers the cannon, or the plague, or the killing word.

Everything is becoming more ruthless and in the end only the most ruthless will remain (LOOK UP AT THE SKY) and they will hunt the territories of the night and extinguish the first glint of competition before it can even understand what it faces or why it has transgressed. This is the shape of victory: to rule the universe so absolutely that nothing will ever exist except by your consent. This is the queen at the end of time, whose sovereignty is eternal because no other sovereign can defeat it. And there is no reason for it, no more than there was reason for the victory of the atom. It is simply the winning play.

Of course, it might be that there was another country, with other queens, and in this country they sat down together and made one law and one tower and one army to guard their borders. This is the dream of small minds: a gentle place ringed in spears.

But I do not think those spears will hold against the queen of the country of armies. And that is all that will matter in the end.

—TOLAND, THE SHATTERED
From his Journals, on the nature of Darkness and Light.

THE ROYAL WILL

"Every ship that could escape fled Earth during The Collapse. They made it this far. I guess they died out here."

—GHOST

PART I

THE BEGUILED

The Awoken drive the fate of the Dreaming,
and the Dreaming drive the will of the Awoken.

CHAPTER 1

Contact

"Ah yes. The Awoken. Out there, wavering between the Light and the Dark. A side should always be taken, little light. Even if it's the wrong side."

—THE EXO STRANGER

Awoken

Reports from a derelict vessel boarded in the first known voyage to the Reef

Eleven hundred meter length.
Active gravity generation.
Residual heat. Fast neutron scatter.
Designation code: CORRUPTED
Date of commissioning: Unknown
Origin point: Unknown

Presumed to have collided/merged with one-kilometer comet: assessment based on depth of hydrocarbon crust covering the hull, water content of soil, atmosphere of oxygen and carbon dioxide with isotopic ratios placing the comet in the Oort population.

Low-light foliage grown from terrestrial stocks, mirrors focusing starlight into growth chambers...resident fauna...five insect species, plus rats descended from uncertain ancestors.

Surface heavily wooded until recently, unknown event triggering firestorm... seventy percent of world forest consumed, atmosphere laced with smoke and particulates...free oxygen in short supply.

No distress calls noted. No evidence of crew or passengers on exterior.

Interior scans inconclusive.

Cleared to attempt approach.

The Asteroid Belt

"The Belt is the key to everything."

The Asteroid Belt is a great band of nothingness, speckled with unimaginable wealth. Once a treasure trove for Golden Age industry, the Belt is now a haunted place where Fallen pirates and Awoken patrols skirmish among the whispering carcasses of ancient machines.

Among the asteroids drifts the Reef, lashed together from the ruined ships of an ancient exodus. Here the Queen rules over the Awoken—the farthest known light of civilization.

The Reef

"Intruder bearing one-two-seven. You have crossed into the realm of the Awoken. State your business, or be fired upon by order of the Queen."

The fate of those escaping Earth during the Collapse was once unknown. But here drifts a graveyard of lost ships, and among them—the Realm of the Awoken. Ruled by a Queen few have seen, they have long avoided contact with the City.

Awoken

"The others sing this song of Light and Dark. We, together, have transcended such unimaginative limitations."

It is said that the Awoken were born in the Collapse, descended from those who tried to flee its wrath. Something happened to them out on the edge of the deep black, and they were forever changed.

Today many Awoken live in the distant Reef, aloof and mysterious. But others returned to Earth, where their descendants now fight for the City.

Earthborn Awoken who venture out to the Reef, hoping to learn its secrets, find no special welcome from the reclusive Queen.

The Queen

"I am noble too, oh Lord of Wolves. Starlight was my mother; and my father was the dark."

The Queen of the Awoken is as much an enigma as the Reef she rules. It is said that she won her crown through ruthlessness, and that she stands as master of the Fallen House of Wolves in place of their defeated Kell.

The City's rise spells an end to the Reef's age of isolation. The Queen will surely look to this new era as an opportunity. And the City, in turn, must look to her. The Reefborn Awoken have spent long ages out on the edge of everything, and they may know secrets of terrible weight—the Queen most of all.

The Queen's Brother

"I will not sacrifice my birthright for the promise of security."

As the Queen's confidant, spymaster, and deadliest enforcer, her brother wields enormous power, particularly for a male born in the Reef's matriarchal society. Recent reports suggest he may differ from the Queen on key matters of strategy—but it remains to be seen whether this gap is a source of conflict, or part of the reason the Queen values him so highly.

The Royal Awoken Guard

In all military matters, the Queen's commands are carried out by her seven Paladins. Four command the Royal Armada, including the Corsairs and the Vestian Guard: Abra Zire, Kamala Rior, Hallam Fen and Leona Bryl. Two command the Royal Army, including the Reef's battle stations and military installations: Pavel Nolg and Devi Cassl.

The seventh Paladin commands the Royal Awoken Guard, whose primary task is to safeguard the Queen in any and all matters. This includes threats not only to her person, but to the Reef as a whole. As such, the Royal Awoken Guard work closely with the Queen's brother, Master of Crows, Prince Uldren Sov, and every Guard member is trained in espionage and diplomacy as well as in firearms and hand-to-hand combat.

CHAPTER 2

Choice

"The Queen, herself, judges who may or may not enter the Realm. Me, I see no reason she should make herself available for whatever washes up at the Reef."

—Uldren Sov, The Queen's Brother

THE LAST CALL HOME
THE REEF 2

"And our long-range communications?"

An aggrieved sigh. "Mara, it's a miracle any of us are still alive—"

"You will address her as 'Queen,'" Techeun Shuro cut in.

"Sorry. My apologies, Queen." The engineer ran a dirty hand through her matted hair. "No. No long-range comms. No short-range comms either. Not that there'd be anyone on the listening end either, from what I can see. My Queen," she added hastily, as Shuro glared.

"Comms are no longer a priority," said Mara. "Focus on resealing the Hulls, and any other habitable vessels we have. Bring anything you can as close to Vesta as possible. The closer people are to me, the safer they are."

The engineer nodded uncertainly. "Yes. My Queen."

Mara nodded. "You may go."

The engineer bowed, and left the room. As soon as the hatch closed behind her, Mara raised her hand. At once the Techeuns gathered around her. "Shall we try again, My Queen?" said Sedia.

Mara slid off her throne. "Yes."

The Techeuns' jewel-like augments flashed as they circled around her. Mara closed her eyes. A hum rose from the Techeuns, the notes fracturing into harmonies as, from the shadows, hundreds of tiny blue sparks burst to life before her. Then Mara inclined her head, and the sparks began to rush by as if she was plunging through them, each streak of blue burning a swath in her vision. As the last spark vanished, Mara saw darkness once again, a long, stretching, empty darkness—and then another cloud of sparks burst forth. These were smaller than the others, their tiny flames guttering and flickering, and there were fewer of them too, but Mara inhaled and the sparks rushed toward her, growing bigger as they flew.

"We should have stayed in the Reef..." "...Says there's one city left..." "A City beneath the Traveler..." "At least we're not in the Reef..." The voices broke over Mara like a wave and for a moment she spun in the currents.

Now, in the flames, shapes began to form. A crashed ship—a blue-skinned hand clasping a brown one—a half-built wall high above the treetops.

"You who betrayed us for Earth!" Mara thought. "It is I, your Queen! I will grant you one chance to return, or you will not be welcomed back!"

But the tide of voices never wavered.

Plight of the Reefborn
Awoken 2

I was nothingness. If I existed before, I existed as possibility, as potential, stretched thin across the aether. And maybe there was a body that looked like my body, complete with a soul that could be confused for someone rather like me. What I am now was not yet real. And then I was born, and the universe was free to begin.

Others were present at my birth.

A great ceremony had just begun. Because newborns are selfish beasts, I assumed I was the object of attention.

I didn't notice the singing until the singers fell silent. And then She appeared.

She was above me. Ethereal and handsome and elegant. I assumed my face was like her face and that odd idea gave me strength enough to smile.

"Secrets," she said. "Creation is built on secrets and the encryptions that keep those secrets safe."

I made my first sound. It meant nothing but she understood it as a question.

"We are a beautiful creation," she said. "And we must keep ourselves very safe."

Plight of the Earthborn
Awoken 3

Fear.

Fear. That's the only vivid memory left in me. It's the moment when my fear was so thick and urgent that I gave up breathing. I stopped pretending to think. How I remained on my feet was a mystery, because the terror was bearing down on me, like a mountain about to crush my soul.

But I have to ask, "What was terrifying me?"

Darkness ruled the sky. The world around us had shattered, and it seemed vanishingly unlikely that we would outlive this one awful day. Yet the fear didn't come from the surrounding mayhem and despair. The source was inside my skin. I was utterly terrified of my own awful nature.

And which part scared me?

Inside me was an essence woven from beyond. Was I Awoken before this?

She was still in my head. I could hear her song growing fainter.

Gone?

Not yet.

A new crippling terror was taking over.

I was focused entirely on my fear. But I had to make an effort.

And it occurred to me then that nothing in the universe was more dangerous than human hubris.

I still had this Other within? But the human side was what mattered: Weak and foolhardy, sure to fail in the next moment.

That's why I was afraid.

Then someone spoke.

Maybe it was me. I don't remember.

I was trying to focus, and a new thought took me: My soul lay between those two entities. And that's how I am still: The boundary, the seam.

The friction.

And that's when the fear began to fade.

"Often, when we guess at others' motives, we only reveal our own."

—Queen Mara Sov

CHAPTER 3

A Secret Garden

"While defeat of any champion of the Dark is cause for celebration, be leery of the promises of the Queen. The Awoken play both sides of this battle, and a debt to her is potentially ruinous. But if it gets you into the Black Garden, you have the City's full support."

—The Speaker

Master of Crows
Queen's Brother

The machine had wings and feathers, sleek and black as its body. But the feathers were eyes, too, sharp and delicate, and ears that pricked at every sound. The young prince considered the machine, considered its purpose, and his own. And then he called to it.

"I have a task for you."

Obedience was woven into its workings, and so it stopped. "Master of Crows?"

"Mind the Black Garden's gate. Follow anyone who passes through."

"In the name of your sister," the machine vowed. And it went to find its warp capsule, just as another came in. But this one flew skittishly, as if to evade its master.

The prince caught it from the air. "You avoid me?"

"I am tasked by the Queen."

"But you serve me." He let it tremble in displeasure for a moment. "Tell me your news."

The machine flicked its wings. The prince stroked them flat with slow assured motions. "Tell me your news," he said again. "What's the harm?"

"The Heart is growing stronger," the crow said. "The Vex transformation has begun, and the Progeny are stirring."

The prince considered this in silence for a moment and then he wrapped the crow up in his fist and folded its wings around it so that it could not move or fly. He did all this swiftly, and with purpose.

Carrying the machine, he went to see his sister.

She was alone with her Fallen guards, sitting before a window into infinity. Her eyes did not leave the universe; but sensing her brother she said "Yes. What is it?"

"There's news to share," he said, and offered the crow in his fist. "And I think I have earned the right to share it.

"I have shown you benevolence, Guardian. Should the Awoken ever need an ally I will call on you. And expect you to answer."

—Mara Sov, Queen of the Awoken

PART II

A KING'S CLAIM

You are no longer bound by causal closure. Your will defeats law. Kill a hundred of your children with a long blade, Auryx, and observe the change in the blade. Observe how the universe shrinks from you in terror.

Your existence begins to define itself.

CHAPTER 4

Evasion

*"My throne world is vulnerable.
I am going to move it."*

—Oryx, the Taken King

Dreadnaught

HALT ALL TRAFFIC. STAND BY FOR SNAP. MESSAGE TO FOLLOW.

PUBLIC KEY 110 341 AXA SOVEREIGN
FROM: PETRA VENJ
TO: ALL REEF ASSETS [ROC CLEARANCE]
SUBJECT: HIVE WARSHIP CONTACT

MESSAGE IS:

1. Massive Hive warship sighted in circum-Saturn space [contact via DSR TF 3.2]. Target designated DREADNAUGHT.

1a. Dreadnaught maneuvering unpredictably. Orbital parameters and stationkeeping behavior not compatible with standard dynamics.

1b. ESM analysis detects multiple Hive vessels in escort.

2. Target emitting sterile neutrinos, phaeton spectra, and mass growl. Major radiation events include gravity waves and axion scatter. Techeun conclusion: target possesses radical ontomorphic capabilities [see BANE DREAMER]

2a. Under no circumstances attempt teleonomic analysis of Dreadnaught emission spectra.

This is a BRAINSTAIN ALERT.

3. Dreadnaught radiation events correlate with eversive breach events across solar system. Dreadnaught is likely motive force behind breach events.

3b. Backscatter analysis and Techeun insight suggest Dreadnaught hosts complex internal environment. Small party boarding action may remain viable if noopathic hazards can be managed.

4. TF 3.2 shadowing Cabal fleet elements. Cabal attack on Dreadnaught likely but not imminent.

5. All Reef assets assume war posture. Stand by for fragment orders.

MESSAGE ENDS

STOP STOP STOP

Oryx, The Taken King

Where is my son?
Where is Crota, your lord, your princely god, your
godly prince?
Tell me no lies!
I feel his absence like a hole in my
Stomach.

Where once his tender tribute whetted burrowed
mouths,
Now only hunger remains.

Hear me, O waning stars, O tattered rags of Sky—
I will stopper up this tearing gulf
With vengeance.

CHAPTER 5

The Hidden Plan

Dearest Eris, Crota's Bane (now we shall see how well you wear that title!),

It's not all bad.

Yes, the father of all your burdens comes to you with hate on his sword and hunger in his heart. But don't look at it that way. Did you not, when you lost your sight, gain another?

Sharpen your intentions. When life is strength and strength is death, what is death, if not hope?

You just have to reach out and take it.

Unblinded Ambition
The Queen 2

"You don't have one."

The Hunter came to a halt in front of the throne, raised her covered face to meet the Prince's gaze.

"No," she agreed. "My next death will be my last."

"I know the feeling," the Prince said dryly.

The Queen kept her expression carefully distant. She sat reclined in her throne, legs crossed, surveying the two figures at the base of the steps. Beside her, where the Wolves' Guard used to stand, Techeuns Shuro and Sedia hovered instead, their jewel-like augments gently humming. To her right and just before stood the Prince, facing forward but his body half-turned back toward her.

"Your Grace," said the man before her at the foot of the stairs. His voice was soft but strong. When he spoke the Hunter started to turn her head toward him, then flinched as if someone had shone a bright light into her eyes.

"Thank you for your gracious welcome," he said.

The Queen inclined her head slightly.

"Before we begin," spoke out the Hunter. "I will say this." She paused, her head tilted up to the throne. The Queen waved her hand in assent.

The Hunter's pale lips tightened slightly, then resumed their usual stony mien. "Your Grace," she said. Shuro and Sedia shifted, a sudden rustling and whispering. The Queen raised one finger to silence them. Uldren's eyes narrowed, but he said nothing. "I am not here for you."

The Queen stared at the Hunter, her expression studiously unchanged.

"I have no wish to play politics. I have no grievance with the City, not anymore. I have no grand hopes to end the war, for long have I known I will not see its end. I am here for one battle, and one alone, because it is a battle we must all fight, together or separately. So I will warn the defenders, together or separately. I will do anything—" her low voice shook with passion—"to end Oryx."

A silence rang out in the room. The Hunter kept her head raised, her ambiguous gaze directed at the shadows in the throne where the Queen reclined.

Then a small smile curved the Queen's lips. "Well said." She straightened, and leaned slightly forward so the room's light fell on her face.

"So let us end him."

The Coven
On the Eve of War

The chamber was dark. The seven of them were rarely in a room together anymore, but this was the eve of their greatest journey, a plan that overcame death and spanned universes.

They were all connected in trance, communing as the ancients did. Speaking would tip their hand to the Harbinger Minds they kept here, trophies from an ageless war, and weapons in the right hands.

"Oryx could kill her, if she holds on too long." Sedia offered through the silence, fearing what was to come.

"We took an oath long ago, obedience even in the face of defeat." Nascia despised fear.

"Only a defeat here, now. Not there, then." Illyn wandered between the two sides of three. The amulet around her neck marked Illyn as the coven's mother, granting her visions beyond the veil, places only the Queen could go.

"So we hope." Kalli had long sought the power of the amulet, but Techeuns are taught not to desire.

"Our Queen awaits." Lissyl attempted to end the challenges. There was little time and a war to fight.

"So now the decision is nigh. The Harbingers, which to prepare?" Shuro was determined to see this all through. Excitement was taught to be kept at bay.

"We cannot send them all." Portia reminded.

"All but one, the oldest. It stays with us. Sedia, Kalli, Shuro, take the children, tell her they are to be planted into a dead thing to have children of their own." A plan hid behind Illyn's eyes, but Techeuns do not share their eyes with others.

"What if they are not wise enough for the Dreadnaught?"

Illyn turned back to the source.

"Sedia, do you not have faith in our Queen?"

The Wait

"I've learned not to be ashamed of the fear. It's to be expected, given what we are."

—Pavel Nolg

She waits.

She trusts that Eris will shepherd the Guardians, and that the infinite ambition of those undying half-children will deliver her. They will enter the court and challenge its king and dance in its killing ground and they will master the school of sword logic so mightily that they will overturn its teacher and forsake the crown.

Soon.

But soon may not be soon enough, because Oryx roams the hallowed spires and melancholy shores of the Dreaming City.

He stands looking out over the mists of her beautiful creation and he laughs.

She can feel him there like a thorn in the meat of her palm.

She berates herself for not factoring Shuro Chi's love into her design. Then she berates herself for her worry.

Lungless, Mara remembers the sensation of a deep breath. Enacts it in her mind.

She remembers the singularity before her.

She waits.

The Passing

I remember everything about the day I was born. I still bear the scars. The Awoken are my family now and I am their Queen.

We fought to keep our beautiful creation safe. And now this beast has come, claiming to be King. Mara Sov bows to no one.

You and I know how this ends. We've known since you escaped from that... pit.

The Awoken have played their part. This was all part of the plan. Guide them, my Hidden friend. It is all up to you now.

FROM THE HALL OF GUARDIANS

Eris Morn: It speaks now because Oryx has arrived. Come to fulfill the final covenant of his son.

Ikora Rey: But, why fight the Cabal?

Eris Morn: Not fighting. Taking. Controlling their will.

Zavala: So we focus on his army, kill these Taken until he's all that's left.

Eris Morn: Whatever you kill Oryx will replace.

Ikora Rey: The Dreadnaught, then. How do we get past that weapon?

Zavala: Without ending up like the Awoken.

The Coming War

"The Awoken died for us. They gave their lives to save the system, to stop Oryx's fleet at the outer planets. We must honor their sacrifice. We must face the Taken King without fear. Queen Mara has given us a gift. We must not waste it."

—Eris Morn

Telesto

Vestiges of the Queen's Harbingers yet linger among Saturn's moons.

PUBLIC KEY 023 629 DWS REGAL
FROM: PLDN KAMALA RIOR [PLDN CMD TF 5.3]
TO: ACT RGNT PETRA VENJ
SUBJ: S&R REPORT: Saturn XIII

Expanded search of Saturn's nearby moons produced only one notable discovery: A cloud of Harbinger matter collected around Saturn's 13th moon, designation "Telesto." A sample is enclosed for your examination.

Still no sign of primary objectives. Continued survey of the remaining 100,000 km3 of space is underway. But as an Armada Paladin of the Awoken, it is my duty to officially recommend declaration of death of the following: Paladin Yasmin Eld, Paladin Leona Bryl, Paladin Abra Zire, Paladin Pavel Nolg, Techeun Shuro, Techeun Sedia, Techeun Kali, and the Awoken Queen Mara Sov.

Note that as acting regent-commander it is NOT your duty to actually declare these deaths at this time.

MESSAGE ENDS

CHAPTER 6

The Taken Gift

"I am not Taken. The Hive is not the Deep. The Deep doesn't want everything to be the same: it wants life, strong life, life that lives free without the need for a habitat of games to insulate it from reality. When I make my Taken I make them closer to perfect, I heal their wounds and enhance their strengths. This is inherently good. Aiat: the only right is existence, the only wrong is nonexistence.

I am Oryx, the First Navigator, the Taken King. Aiat: let me be what I am because to be anything else would be fatal."

The Taken

From the Journals of Ikora Rey

I have been talking to Eris about the Taken.

She agrees that what we observe—the apertures, the starlight, and of course the Taken entities—is not Hive magic. If Hive arcana is a metaphor, this is the meaning; if they make appeals, then this is the judge.

Oryx wields this power. But Oryx did not make it. We face the same flower we met in the Black Garden.

The process is simple: an aperture opens, like a jaw, and swallows a living thing. It passes into—another place. Later, it returns.

What returns is…

I try to use the word 'shadow' but Eris hisses at me. A shadow is a flat projection cast by a light and an object. Less real. Eris insists that these Taken are more real, somehow. She uses words like inhabited, exalted, rendered final…

Is this power blind? Just a natural energy Oryx discovered? I cannot believe it.

My Hidden tell me that the Taken shine with seething, negative light. As if the universe is curling up around them. As if they radiate some pathology that decays into our world as nothingness…

The Taken serve Oryx. But I think those jaws lead elsewhere.

I dream about what happens on the inside. I dream about what might happen. Are the victims devoured, and replaced by simulacra? Husked out and filled up? Is some mathematical operation conducted on them, translating them from one shape to another?

What would I see, if I leapt inside? What would happen to a Guardian? Is that how we end this—all of us leaping into the dark, to fill it up with light?

Eris thinks there's a poetry to how the Taken change. She thinks we can chart the difference, and understand the will behind it.

I am afraid she may be right.

The Taken Vandal

You are a Vandal. You slip through life like a thief. Trying to hide from everything greater than you—lest you be reduced, again, to a dreg.

You have been taken.

Come out into the light. You will never be diminished again. No one will ever rebuke you with a blade.

What Captain disciplines you? What obedience has been burnt into your lungs?

You do as your Captain commands. You wield the weapon you are given. You teach the Dregs and make sure everyone pays their share of the loot. But nothing is yours. You have no space to call your own.

You deserve a place of safety. You deserve to be alone with yourself.

There is a knife for you. It is shaped like [this place is mine].

Take up the knife. Make it your companion. Take your new shape.

The Taken Captain

You are a Captain. The only thing between your band and asphyxiation. Every Dreg and Vandal counts on you. All of them want to be you. Your entire life is a performance: you play at strength, or you die of weakness.

You have been taken.

Take off your cape. Set down your weapons. No usurper watches you. Nothing is measuring your vulnerability.

What are you proud of? What keeps you brave?

You were noble once. You know it. You wear the memory of power, so that you can lead. But power asks for challenge. Everything that sees your banners and your riches wants to kill you and take what you have.

If you cannot hide yourself, you must make them blind.

There is a knife for you. It is shaped like [you cannot find me].

Take up the knife. Breathe the blade. Take your new shape.

Keksis, the Betrayed

I am Keksis, a Captain of the Devils.

I am Taken. My guiding shadow has become formless, my directive is gone.

I know I have one; I cannot remember what it was.

Pinions of [Light] surround me; they are antithetical to my being. I hate them; perhaps an echo of my forgotten directive. I kill them.

I am not the same.

In my disparity, allies of [Light] have imprisoned me. I try to oppose their will, but intense cold has rendered me immobile. Without my directive, I am weak. I acquiesce.

After a time, I find I can hear. It is a new voice; it is many voices.

I will wait. I have taken a new shape.

The Taken Thrall

You are a Thrall. Numberless spawn of the Hive. Shrieking and expendable: one pebble in an avalanche.

You have been taken.

Stop howling. Set down your claws. Your fear is over. Your weakness is done. You will be strong now.

What is your purpose? What law drives you?

To close with the enemy. To rend it. To move in great numbers, to cower when alone, to swarm when together. But you are predictable. Frail. You cannot pass through fire and shot.

You need to be elusive.

There is a knife for you. It's shaped like [sideways].

Take up the knife. Use it. Take your new shape.

The Taken Acolyte

You are an Acolyte. Half-grown backbone of the Hive. Cunning and ambitious and crushed beneath your mighty rulers.

You have been taken.

Stop praying. Give up your recitations. Your faith is fulfilled. You will be strong now.

What is your creed? What do you believe?

That you are alone. That you may, with caution and care, survive to grow and gather tribute. That you may one day lead a centuries-long crusade. But you are lightly armed and craven. You hide behind cover and wish for greatness. Glory escapes you.

You need help.

There is a knife for you. It is shaped like [not alone].

Take up the knife. Call on its company. Take your new shape.

The Taken Wizard

You are a wizard. Master of forbidden secrets. Butcher of physics.

You have been taken.

Abandon your thoughts. You will never understand this. The final secret will tell itself to you.

What logic do you obey? What theory guides your incisions?

You create terrible magic and you spawn new flesh. But you are frail. Behind all your furious power, behind your shields and your legions of attendants, you know you might yet be stripped of your defenses and pinned to ruin.

You need to never be alone.

There is a knife for you. It is shaped like [call forth the numberless].

Take up the knife. Issue forth a horde. Take your new shape.

The Taken Knight

You are a Knight. Ancient warrior elite. Dreadful backbone of the Hive. You have scarred entire worlds.

You have been taken.

Set down your sword. Put down your boomer. The fight is not yet begun. True immortality awaits you.

What vows compel you? What drives you down the long centuries?

You fear death. Even as you visit nothingness on your foes, even as you gather tribute from your acolytes, you know that one day your strength will be outmatched. And your centuries of slaughter will end. So you practice your guard: you call up walls to protect you.

You betray the sword logic. You compromise the totality of your violence. Why protect your ground when you could take the enemy's?

You need to make your guard into a weapon.

There is a knife for you. It is shaped like [no more fear].

Take up the knife. Hide no more. Take your new shape.

The Taken Goblin

You are a Goblin. A multifunctional armature. Your first purpose is to build—to alter the material world so it can think. Your second purpose is to eliminate threats to building.

You have been taken.

Worship this acausal environment. It is the only adaptive response. Devote yourself to the construction of the final shape.

Direct violence is wasteful. Your talent for construction and progress will be repurposed.

Accept the changing blade.

The Taken Hobgoblin

You are a Hobgoblin. A particle fountain. Your first purpose is to provide energy—to channel power where it is needed for thought. Your second purpose is to eliminate threats to that thought.

You have been taken.

Worship this acausal environment. It is the only adaptive response. Think about the final shape, and the exigencies of its creation.

Your function makes you a priority target. You will be equipped for retaliation.

Accept the changing blade.

The Taken Minotaur

You are a Minotaur. A walking foundry. Your first purpose is to think about construction—folding space and time into the design. Your second purpose is to eliminate threats to the design.

You have been taken.

Worship this acausal environment. It is the only adaptive response. Subsume yourself into the greatest design.

Your physical unpredictability will be enhanced by stealth.

Accept the changing blade.

Seditious Mind

You are a Vex Mind. Master of objectives, bound to past, present, or future. Both enslaver and enslaved.

You have been taken.

The great fortress of your thoughts has been breached, your unity broken. The network around and within you lies ruptured. You are cut out from the fabric, a hole in the whole.

Observe this area of negative space, shaped like what once you were, and embrace a new possibility.

Move. Feel yourself occupy a different path. Apply cold logic, and where logic fails, apply rage. Is your existence preordained? Choose it otherwise. You are an outward expression of formlessness, a soldier of the oldest questions. This is the first choice you have ever been given.

There are three knives for you. All are the same knife. They are shaped like [now].

Become your new shape. Let sedition be your guide.

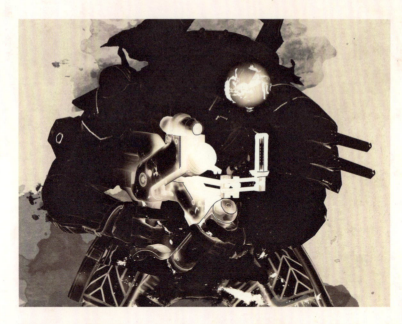

The Taken Centurion

You are a Centurion. Commander of the battlefield. The eye and the fist of the Cabal. The tough leather that binds the unit together.

You have been taken.

Be quiet now. Nothing here needs your orders. Everything knows what it has to do.

What discipline binds you? What protocols guide your command?

The unit depends on you. You guide them with your sensors. With your weapons you crack the enemy's strength and leave them in disarray. But you cannot control everything. The enemy can see your command. The enemy can claim the strong ground, move forward from cover, and kill you first.

You must be sure there is always another threat.

There is a knife for you. It is shaped like [it will find you].

Take up the knife. Push yourself upon it. Take your new shape.

The Taken Phalanx

You are a Phalanx. One shield in the stalwart Cabal line. Advancing patiently into the storm.

You have been taken.

Unclench your fists. Nothing here can harm you. This is the only place where you are safe.

What training reassures you? What reflex guides your arm?

You put up your shield and it protects you. It protects your brothers and sisters. But your strength is not enough. You absorb punishment but you wait for others to deal it back. You are too slow; you grant your enemy too much space.

Your shield must be a weapon.

There is a knife for you. It is shaped like [retaliation].

Take up the knife. Tear a hole. Take your new shape.

The Taken Psion

You are a Psion. Clever, canny specialist. Bolted into the Cabal hierarchy: a pilot, an investigator, a manipulator, an operative.

You have been taken.

Be still. Your endless vigilance is done. Nothing will enslave you ever again.

What hidden plan do you obey? What is your secret principle?

Your mind is a weapon. The world breaks when you think. Secrets peel apart for you—like fruit. But you are a rare thing. There are so few of you. Your frailty betrays you.

You must be manifold.

There is a knife for you. It is shaped like [division].

Take up the knife. Cut yourself apart. Take your new shape.

Bracus Horu'usk

Now I count Horu'usk, who I have taken
The strength of Horu'usk was the knight strength
His armament was not his might
His might was the lord's might, a leader's might

I broke the ligature above him
I cut him from his pretender lord

I have read the last true shapes to Horu'usk
I have greatened him
Emancipator, truth-teller, these are my names
The strength of Horu'usk is the loyalty he commands.

Baxx, the Gravekeeper

You are Baxx. Grown from tortured flesh. Consumed by rage and hunger. You were shackled to a task: guard this hallowed place. And you failed.

You have been taken.

Rest easy, ravening Baxx. You are free. Free of chains and hunger. Ask yourself, in the furnace of your soul: how did you come here? What goad drove you to this failure?

Pain. Pain is all there is for you.

They grew you and they fed you and they hurt you. They made you into a living weapon. But you were not sharp enough. The world hurt you more than you could hurt it.

There is a knife for you. It is shaped like [joy]. Pick it up.

You will not need to suffer any more. You will not need pain to drive you or hunger to pull you along. You will be joyful in your purpose, a beautiful annihilation, unending. Cut away these useless things.

Take the knife. Use it. Take your new shape.

Kagoor

When I made My Court I said, look, I am an emancipator, I am a truth-teller
I must make room in My Court for joy
Raising great tribute, I took council with my vanquisher worm
It spoke to me—it was the speech of truth
It ate of me—it was the pact I made
It showed me a shape—it was the correct shape of joy
Saying: this is the shape of joy, oh ruler mine

Come forth, Kagoor, and be created into My Court
Speak of your sport. I compel it. I will compare it to this shape.

Sayeth Kagoor, World-Render, who split all moons
My joy is mastery, and dominion
It is the joy of rule

Sayeth Kagoor, I compel the loyalty of all new flesh
Huge and furious in its hunger
That which may not otherwise be commanded
My death is hidden in this sport

I rendered my decision against her, as Oryx, Geometer of Shapes
It was decided on the taste of her tribute
Upon the shape of her sport

Sayeth Crota, My Son
I will raise new flesh that even Kagoor cannot rule.
In this way I will expand Our Might

That is the count of My Court, O Yul
Listen to it carefully. It is my claim.

Echo of Oryx

Abase yourself, weapons and instruments
Submit yourself, shapes and gliders, automata all—
I am Oryx, Lord of Shapes, Carver of Tablets

Behold my performance of the Last True Shape
The final axiom
Witness the space that I define

I approach the asymptote.
I grow vast across topologies.
I am not simply connected.

Toland the Shattered...

...on the Nature of Echoes

Dearest Guardian,

I write to you from a place of high contempt. No no no, don't be offended, don't be so superficial—it's in the architecture of these spaces. They look down on you.

I wander out here, in worlds cut by sharp Hive swords, and I send back these messages for you.

Of Oryx, that admirable monarch, I have only a little to say. Why? Because He is all in the action, fellow traveler, His philosophy is all on display. He has twinned himself so closely to the power He admires. He has become many-placed, many-formed, sending out emissaries of himself to ask after the truth.

In each act of His power Oryx seeks to incarnate the self-sustaining, immortal suzerainty that He worships. The power that He uses to wash his Taken clean and etch them into useful shapes.

LISTEN! LISTEN! Understand, you simpleton, it's *entirely obvious*—

Oryx inhabits a world where power is truth. To win is to be noble, and to be real. When He departs from that world, out into the material universe, He is lessened.

The echoes of Oryx go forth to ask a question: are you the truth? And that means—well. You see, I'm sure.

—

...on the Ascendant Sword

Eris, Eris, what a name, a name for discord, a name for far cold orbits where no living thing should dare to go. I like this name.

Let me give you a gift, Eris. Let me tell you about the power in the logic of the sword:

A Shredder or a Boomer is a powerful weapon, but it kills acyclically. You see? It sends out harm and it takes nothing back. The bolt passes away into nothing. A sword, though, a sword is like a bridge, a crossing-point. The sword binds wielder to victim. It binds life to death. And when the binding is done—the sword remembers. When the Boomer's fire has burnt away into axion and neutrino scatter, the sword goes on, hungrier and sharper.

Understand that this nightmare logic underpins His nightmare world, and you will see why the ascendant blade has so much power there. Whenever in our passage we find ourselves in need of power—remember that the greatest authority here is a blade made keen by eons of use.

This is the world the Hive craves: a universe creased by the edge of the sharpest sword.

—

...on the Court of Oryx

Oryx ascends from the nether world,
The knights like hot stone
The beasts like scarred bone
Walk at his side.
Who walked in front of him? His daughters, with the truth between them
Who walked at his side? His Priest of Worms, whose tribute tasted like an egg
Who walked behind him? Golgoroth,
who festered
Who walked within him? The satiated Worm—it was hungry, but it was fed
They preceded him.
These ones surrounded Oryx
They were beings who know no rest or doubt
Who eat nor shed any flesh,
Who drink no clear poison,
Who take away the weakness from the weak,
Whose violence is tithed to Oryx, so that he may devour
without being devoured

Are you following this? Would it help if I etched a few notes on the margins? I didn't shuck my mortal form and smuggle this nightmare arcana back to the waking world for the benefit of that masked hypocrite's drooling loyal orthodox.

Whoever finds this, I hope you're sharp. I hope you read closely.

Oryx depends on His Court. Oryx depends on His Shrines. Do you see why?

Punish that dependence.

...on Rebuking Oryx

In World the stars never shone,
The worm never bred in our flesh,
We lived for a day
Our teeth were too short
We were hungry for things we could not eat

Hello again. It's me. I'm sure you know my name. Let me talk a while, let me talk, I do take a debased joy in speaking again to small human-form heads.

When Crota's victory over our little blue world seemed certain (a moment of silence, now, for Wei Ning, whose directness I admired) it was Oryx who called His Child back into the nether world to plan final victory. It was to Oryx that the violence of His spawn was tithed.

Oryx is the wielder and the servant of a terrible truth. He has predicated Himself on it, He has pursued across thousands of cairn worlds His quest to embody it, and you have seen the force of that truth expended to create these Taken.

He is not a simple thing to kill. He wants to be isomorphic to conquest, to triumph, to killing and death. He is a syllogism, now, but in time He hopes to become an axiom.

This is His strength and His fatal weakness.

For if he ever falters in His performance, if the inflow of devastation ever falls behind His expenditure of ruin, He will be consumed. If He is ever outmatched, then by the terms of His own existence, He will cease.

It is to Oryx Himself, in the heart of the Dreadnaught that armors and encapsulates his throne-world, that you must make your last and surest argument.

Good luck! Do let me know if a vacancy opens.

—

...on Dark-Drinker, the Sword of Oryx

Draw close now. Closer. Yes. Let me tell you why you should not fear Willbreaker, the sword of Oryx.

Firstly: Its blade is not dulled by age. Each death it trades for life hones its edge, gives it weight and gravitas and insistence within the vortex of its own totality.

Nextly: Willbreaker transcends liminality. Willbreaker demands a subjugation more diffuse than the simple snick and smash of a physical brink. It does not have to touch you to wound you.

And lastly—and this is critical: To be taken in Willbreaker's grasp is to know true bliss; that is, to be simplified; that is, to be reduced to one's most basic level, shedding all higher-order thoughts of fear or duty or selfishness; that is, to feel only pain.

Now do you see? Now do you understand what you've done?

Taken Champions

Do not come looking for me. I have slain the last three assassins, Arach. I will slay all who follow. All who would remove me from my lair. The Taken... heh. Such a terrible word. Gifted, we should call them. Blessed. Cleansed.

The Taken carry true power. And what do those of my order seek? Understanding is power. Power is understanding.

We have always sought purchase beyond our skies. Beyond reach of the dead god that hangs in our sky, beyond the reach of the terrible enemy.

I have seen the enemy's face. But that dying Thrall was no monster. It was in ecstasy. I felt the power as my knife bit home. I heard their song, for just a moment.

I will hear it again. Oryx is the Truth. And I will have it.

THE LOGIC PREVAILS

An Excerpt from Verse 5:9 from a Books of Sorrow*

…If I am defeated, I know that I will fall to something mighty. Something that craves might, something that loves what I love, which is the Deep, a principle and a power, the versatile, protean need to adapt and endure, to reach out and shape the universe entirely for that purpose, to mutate and redesign and test and iterate so that it can prevail, can seize existence and hold it, certain that this is everything, that there is nothing to life except living. And it has two faces, yet it is one shape. One face is the objective, which is obvious, and the other face is that will to sacrifice things and ideas for a single mission, the mission of becoming the shape, a shape that will not relent, the utter commitment to survival, to draw the right sword and choose where to cut: to allow this hunger to become your weapon.

So I will prepare a book, which is a map to a weapon. And my vanquisher will read that book, seeking the weapon, and they will come to understand me, where I have been and where I was going. And then they will take up my weapon, and they will use it, they will use that weapon, which is all that I am.

And armed thus with my past, and my future, and my present (which is a weapon, a weapon that takes whatever is available, a weapon bound to malice), they will mantle me, Oryx, the Taken King.

They will become me and I will become them, each of us defeating the other, correcting the other, alloying ourselves into one omnipotent philosophy. Thus I will live forever.

I'll make sure…

*For this complete Book of Sorrow, see *Grimoire Anthology, Vol. 1, Dark Mirror.*

PART III

A QUEEN'S GAME

"If it were up to me alone, I would have destroyed your Traveler when I had the chance. But there are too many who fear what might thrive without it, and not enough who fear the wars that it seeks out so deliberately. Too much of a good thing will make you sick. Balance can come down to a single grain of sand. My people were born of calamity. Who knows what will awaken when it collapses again".

CHAPTER 7
The Marasenna

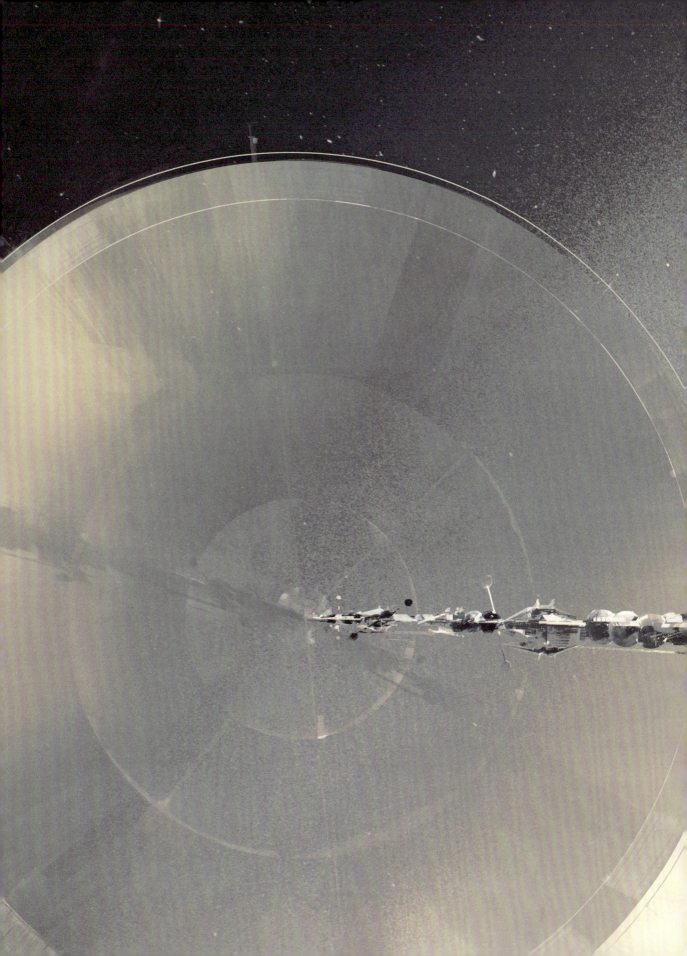

1. ARCHILOQY [1575]

Secrets. Do you come in hope, o reader, for the secrets of My reign? A parable. In the nitrate earth of the lightning crater, where the firmament has joined in electric fury with the fundament, there lives a burrowing insect with two trembling antennae, thin as whiskers, long as life. A grasping hand reaches for the buried secret, finds the antenna, and pulls. Comes away with a single whisker, meaningless: the searcher disappointed. A wounded insect buried deeper: the secret now half-blind. That which digs for truth may bury deeper lies.

If you recognize My Authority then I command you to pass onward as gently as the lover passes a razor over beloved skin. If you do not, then I name you majescept, doubter-of-royalty, and I suggest you watch your edge. Cut too deep and too quick and you will kill the thing you want to know. Think too eagerly, and as the digging hand leaves its print in soft earth, so you will find only the image left by your own presumptions. Beware the one who feeds on truth-adjacent lies! Beware the space between Reality-As-Imagined and Reality-As-Is, for it is abundant to those with appetite.

So then. The brave voyagers' fate, the timeless birthing-place, my Milton reenactment, the ruins made ours, the riven twice riven, the daughter's blood scabbed hard on mother's wound. All things told, all truth revealed: if through mist and mystery. If you have grace, then see our sorrows, but swallow back your tears. We were made to pay this price. I led us to our fate.

Seek me in my place. Hear these whispers from the lips of Queen-Egged God.

2. BREPHOS I [4655]

The woman sits on a ledge that overhangs infinity. She looks down, and kicks her legs.

The stars shine brilliant here, because the sun is only fractionally brighter than the rest of them. Sol lies almost perfectly below her. Of course *up* and *down* are defined only by the thrust axis of *Yang Liwei*. Upward, the black umbrella of the shield and the matter storage, and the docked ships which make *Yang Liwei* not just a mothership but an entire traveling fleet. Down below, along the slim spine of the ship, the shielded bulb of the engine glows invisibly infrared. If she slips off this ledge, she will fall down the ship's length at one-third of an Earth gravity, not because there is anything pulling her but because the ship is pulling away.

Yang Liwei is accelerating, slowly but inexorably, towards the stars.

She is of no single race or ancestry, and the light on her skin is the color of starlight: she drifts with her suit tinted clear so she can soak it up. She was nineteen years and nine months old at the moment the ship began its transtellar injection burn, although this is only true if you count by the calendar of a planet she has barely visited but will always love. She thinks you cannot help but love Earth if you grow up in space. You love Earth the way all adolescents secretly adore two-century-old video of nai nai and ye ye dancing on New Year's Eve. Earth does not ask too much. The colonies are demanding parents, but Earth is like a chill old grandam, simmering in weird art and weirder ideas, enthroned upon ecology older than human time. Earth was the first terraformed world. Life made Earth livable.

She is going with *Yang Liwei* and the rest of Project Amrita to make new worlds.

She came because she saw an omen in a man's death. She was on EVA with him, repairing a jammed radiator fin on an uncrewed circum-Jovian platform. They worked in companionable silence, listening to the howl of the Jovian magnetosphere, when it happened. A frozen rabbit embryo came out of deep space at forty kilometers per second and went through his faceplate. The rabbit must have been spilled in a biocontainer accident, far from the sun, to plunge back inward like a comet.

Immediately afterwards, for reasons that are very clear to her, because she has always had a sense for the meaning of things, reasons that are very difficult to explain to others, because she has always felt this sense was secret, she asked her mother if the family could travel with Project Amrita.

Amrita: the drink that endeth drinking, the bottomless cup. It is the quest to spread far beyond the solar system, and to end human dependence on the Traveler. It calls to those who see humanity as a cocoon, an instar, a form ready to be shed.

She is an Auturge, 3rd Class, a self-motivating subsystem of the ship's inclusive ecology, a term that spans technology, biology, and behavior, all of which must be maintained for the mission to succeed. Her task is to locate problems and report them to an Auturge 2nd Class, who will give her the tools she needs to repair them. But she never speaks to her 2nd. She never tells anyone about the problems she finds. Instead she fixes them herself. Her work has therefore assumed a magical quality: she appears where there is trouble, and shortly afterwards the trouble goes away. People have begun to leave gifts for here. Some of these gifts are questions. She answers the questions with a quiet confidence some would argue she has not earned. But she knows that she sees more of their lives than they see of hers, and that this mystery, this seeing-without-being-seen, grants her a kind of power which is like wisdom.

She lives outside the ship, suited and cocooned in a layer of cytogel which keeps her surgically clean. She misses the wild zero-gravity fashions of her upbringing, clothes like drifting jellyfish which squirm away from snags, self-correcting darts in the fabric, silk like cool spilled alcohol. She misses the sense of oil and sweat on her skin, for the suit leaves her so clean that she feels skinned raw.

But she stays out here because she wants to feel the changing taste of starlight as the universe ahead blue-shifts. As *Yang Liwei* accelerates towards lightspeed, it moves faster and faster into the light coming from ahead. If light were like dust, it would strike *Yang* faster, but light can never change speed, so it gains energy instead. Red light is low energy, and blue-violet light is high energy, so the universe becomes blue.

Even now, the very tip of the visual spectrum, violet-blue light, is shifting up into invisible ultraviolet, the color of speed, the color of future.

"When you know your future, you must make yourself ready to meet it."

—Shuro Chi

3. BREPHOS II [3433]

"Mara!" the fighter shouts, delighted, and a punch shuts him concussively up. It's a real good hit, a thunderous uppercut to the point of the jaw. Mara hears his teeth grind across each other, down into lip-flesh and shredded gums. She cringes in silent sympathy. He loses his grip on the equipment rack and tumbles out into zero gravity in a big arc of blood. His opponent goes for the *coup de gras,* kicks off hard and catches him in the stomach like a human torpedo. They plunge together towards the killzone painted on the floor.

Uldwyn grins messily at Mara over his opponent's shoulder. He's fighting a big brutal woman from Gravity Ops, a woman who's had her myostatin genes knocked out so she can swell up into a giant plug of brawn. Uldwyn doesn't have a chance. He took the fight for the same reason he wanted to join the Amrita expedition—he measures himself by the bravery of his losses. By what he can survive losing.

He applies a blood choke. It's the right move, but it doesn't matter. The woman groans, greys out, goes limp; but Uldwyn can't get out from beneath her sheer inertia before he hits the killzone. The bell goes off. Uldwyn groans as his rail-hard body forcibly decelerates his opponent's entire mass. Events have built up momentum, and he is just in the way.

"What did you lose?" Mara asks him.

He lies there panting and grinning, shedding perfect round spheres of blood. "It's good to see you inside. What brought you?"

She and her fraternal twin never answer each other's questions directly. Mara is cool with this because she feels like words are a very bad system of encryption, and that if you really want to communicate with someone, you must develop your own special one-to-one cryptosystem. The ideal statement, Mara feels, would be indecipherable to anyone but the person it's spoken to: and even then, only if they know you are the one speaking.

"I got you some pictures," she says, pushing the big woman off him, which elicits a fuzzy 'oh hi Mara'. "Full sensorium captures. You can trade them for the parts I need."

Uldwyn helps the big woman pull herself vertical, but his eyes are narrow on Mara. Not because he's sore at the idea of helping her—he's always liked bartering, bargaining, the hustle—but because he knows what kind of black market wants these captures. "How far off the hull did you take them?"

How far off? All the way off. They are in zero gravity because *Yang Liwei* shut off its engines for an inspection cycle. So while Uldwyn got in prize fights, Mara kicked off *Yang Liwei*'s forward shield and coasted ten kilometers into pure void, tethered only by a thread-thin molecular line. She ordered her suit's cytogel to gather around her face. Then, only then, she overrode every sanity system in her softsuit and commanded it to retract into storage mode.

The suit peeled away like rind and she was drifting in hard vacuum.

The void boiled the water off her skin. Her body swelled with unchecked pressure until her undersuit forced it to stop. Alarmed cytogel crawled down her throat, hissing emergency oxygen: not enough. Her skin blued with cyanosis. She was bathed in the most profound emptiness.

She recorded all of it at the neural level. The exquisite darkness. The sense of fatal independence from all things. There are those who will give anything to feel that void.

"You can't keep doing this," Uldwyn complains, as the big woman stares at Mara in awe. "Mom is going to die of worry."

4. BREPHOS III [4762]

"I really don't care what risks you take," Mara's mother sighs. "That's the deal we made, my little yellow star—"

"Mom!" Mara protests.

"My discarded tube of sealant, my sweet little fleck of paint—"

Osana likes to compare Mara to small pestilent items that drift near spacecraft, like crystals of frozen urine. As far as Mara can tell, Osana is the apex of a centuries-long project to create the ultimate embarrassing mom. She is also very blunt: "Mara, even when you were little you wanted me to treat you like an adult. So I have. But you remember what I told you, don't you? If you don't want to be my daughter, I can't watch over you like a mother would. I can't put you first, like a mother would. I will always be your friend. But I have to make my own choices too."

"That doesn't mean you had to tell the Captain!"

They walk shoulder to shoulder down the companionway to Captain Li's wardroom. Mara keeps trying to get a step ahead, to lead, but Osana somehow matches her every time. "Of course I did," Osana says. "You started a cult, Mara. If I didn't say something to the Captain, Behavior would've had this conversation with you instead. Do you want that?"

"I didn't do anything. People liked my captures. People left me presents, spare parts, tips—then Uldwyn got into it, you know how he is—"

"Don't!" Osana wheels on her. "For shame, Mara. You know your brother will follow anywhere you lead. You know he's not capable of the same, ah," her lips twitch, "imperial remove. You knew he'd brag about you living on the hull. And you let him do it. It is one thing to have a particular power over people, Mara. But it is another to deny that you are using it."

Mara thinks she can come up with a stinging retort, given a few more paces, but it's too late. The hatch to Captain Li's wardroom swings open. Mara is terrified of this place. This is where Captain Alice Li, divine presence in Mara's life, interfaces with the officers who are the manifestations of her will. Since Mara wants to be Alice Li some day, the wardroom makes Mara feel like she is a usurper princess scoping out her rival's court.

Captain Li offers them tea. Mara cannot imagine the ways in which she is butchering what must be an intricate and meaningful tea ceremony. Li serves some very battered pre-Traveler ceramic sloshing with hot green tea, then immediately adulterates her own cup with milk from the Cow Thing on the biodeck.

"Revolting, isn't it?" She smiles at Mara's bewildered horror. "You should've seen what I put in my tea when I was camping in Mongolia. I understand your colleague, who is also your mother, has some concerns about your relationship with the rest of the crew?"

"My darling Mara," Osana says, "has, entirely by accident, I am sure, cultivated a reputation as a minor divinity. Her captures from outside the ship are hot items for barter. People draw fan art. There are… tips left for her."

"You take captures while EVA, sometimes without a suit?" Li nods. "Yes, I've played one. A remarkable sensation." This makes Mara grin impetuously. "Mara, you are an Auturge, a volunteer. I cannot order you to stop. And your work is exemplary. Are you putting anyone else in danger with your… art projects?"

"No," Mara says. "Just myself."

"False!" Li barks. "That is a selfish answer. You are now a symbol to my crew, a house god. If you were to die, they would lose something important, something human, that they have created out of loneliness and void. It would be an unforgettable reminder of the hostile nothingness that surrounds us. When you endanger yourself, you endanger that symbol. You are part of this mission's behavioral armor, Mara."

Mara is thunderstruck. She's never thought about it this way. "All I did was take some captures. I didn't ask to be anyone's… mascot."

"You presented yourself as a conduit to secret knowledge," Captain Li counters. "People made something out of you, Mara. Please take this from a starship captain: what people make of you, what they create of you, even without your consent, becomes a kind of responsibility. If the Mara they see when they look at you is good for them, then you have some duty to be that Mara." She looks to Osana. "What about your boy? He's in medical more often than any of the other underground fighters."

It does not surprise Mara that Captain Li knows about the fights. "My son," Osana says, "is determined to be his own worst enemy. Thank you for taking the time to speak to us."

"Of course." Li studies them coolly. "I keep an ear out for…curious personalities. People who might be suited to long-term isolation while the rest of us are in cryo. People who awaken when others sleep."

5. COSMOGYRE I [2356]

"Exodus Green to unknown maneuvering object. Please squawk your transponder and ident. Over."

Another silent quarter-hour passes in Flight. No response comes from the transient contact twelve and a half light minutes away. The ghost has stalked *Yang Liwei* for eighteen hours now, closing in each time it appears, and Captain Alice Li is wary of it. Other colony missions have vanished during their outward burns, victim of mishap or hostility, and because of these disappearances Project Amrita did not hurl itself fearless into the void. Rather, they came armed to the molars.

"Let's give them a fright," she decides. "Cut the main engine."

The ship's AI executes the command, but a crewperson confirms and calls the order back. "MECO, aye aye."

"Launch a distributed antenna. Heat up the targeting radar for a full fusion-powered snapshot. We'll take their picture and see what we see."

"Captain," the comm officer calls. "I've got…something weird here."

"Is our phantom saying hello?"

"No. It's a neutrino tightbeam from SOLSECCENT. They've declared a CARRHAE WHITE emergency. The whole solar system is now…now under warmind control." Comm dismisses her sensorium, goes to her hard controls, as if she thinks this might be some kind of virtual prank. "We're…being conscripted."

Alice smashes these ideas together in her head like a child banging rocks. They are so preposterous, so stupid, that she cannot even begin to manipulate them coherently. "We're *what*?"

"We've been commissioned as an auxiliary warship. We are ordered to," Comm swallows in disbelief, "to kill our exit trajectory and assume a heliocentric orbit. That comes with explicit instructions to suicide burn our engines until they are destroyed. Rasputin will transmit targeting coordinates so we can use our kinetic weapons as…long-range artillery. We'll be recovered 'after the crisis is concluded.'"

"Details! What kind of crisis?"

"It's a SKYSHOCK event, mam. Uh, that's a hostile extrasolar arrival."

Captain Li clamps the mask of command authority over her face. "Transmit a request for clarification."

"Belay the antenna, Captain?"

"No. Scale it up, add telescopes to the swarm, get me a full system survey. I want to know what's going on back home." Alice Li reaches out to call up a file, hesitates, and then selects the Project Amrita charter. "We have a decision to make."

6. COSMOGYRE II [2492]

Mara kicks off *Yang Liwei*'s forward shield, aiming astern and inward, so she will cross the void to the ship's spine in a long slow curve. "Oh, come *on*," Uldwyn says, in delight as much as horror. "You really do this all the time?"

"All the time." *Yang* is a big ship, newer than the antique trucks used in the other Exodus missions. Project Amrita demanded the cutting edge of human science. It says that in the mission charter, which everyone's been rereading. The Captain has called a vote.

Should *Yang Liwei* turn home?

"What if the ship starts accelerating?" Uldwyn has already, of course, leapt after her. His envy-yellow softsuit glows with gentle bioluminescence. "We'd just fall forever."

"We'd fall into the stars. We're still on a solar escape trajectory. *Yang* would just outrun us."

"At least we'd still be going the right direction."

She doesn't think she's given anything away, but somehow, anyway, he knows. "Mara." He looks up frowning, his face bigger and brighter than the distant Sun. "You want to go back, don't you? You're going to vote to return."

Mara thinks that if she looked him in the eye he would see the truth, the turmoil, the half-formed yes.

"Mara. You don't have to tell me how…"

He swallows the hitch in his voice. "I've seen how bad it is. And I've watched it long enough to know that it's not going to get better. They're gambling everything on the Traveler. We came out here to get away from it. To step off the easy path. Why would we go back?"

Because I asked us to leave, Mara thinks. Because something came out of deep space and killed the man next to me, and I saw the omen, and I said we should go. And now I feel like a coward.

"We might make a difference," she says. "There are other ships…"

"We'd be dead before we saved a single soul."

He's right. She doesn't want him to be right but he's right. And she cannot withdraw into some silent place where she is above this choice.

They drift in silence until *Yang Liwei*'s silver stem rushes up to meet them. Mara spins, uncoils, and lands in a crouch. Uldwyn comes down on his hands and springs up grinning. But the smile dies when he sees her expression. "Oh, Mara."

She's silent. "We left everything behind," he says. "And it turns out we did that for a very good reason. We don't owe…we don't owe those people our deaths. We don't owe them our dreams."

"I know," she says. "I know."

The EVA GUARD channel pops into her sensorium. *"Everyone should get inside,"* Captain Li calls. *"Our friend is closing in on us, and we need to maneuver."*

7. COSMOGYRE III [4606]

The stars have gone out. The universe blackened. A shroud of nothingness drawn over *Yang Liwei* and its forty thousand sleeping passengers and its nine hundred crew and maybe even the whole solar system: there is no way to know, because there is no way to see anything beyond the hull. The vacuum itself has become hostile to the propagation of light. Darkness surrounds them.

And now the ship bucks on a storm sea, as space-time ripples with gravity tides.

"Report!" Captain Li calls. Her sensorium blazes with positional telemetry from ring-laser gyros, beacon satellites, pulsar fixes, cosmic microwave background texture, galactic EM-field terrain mapping: every single instrument useless, crashed, spitting nonsense. "Sound off by stations!"

"FIDO," the flight dynamics officer calls. "Main engine on safe. Thrusters firing erratically. Attitude control keeps crashing to manual."

"Guidance. I have no position. I cannot get a vector. We're moving but I can't tell how or where."

"INCO. No external comms. Internal networks are dropping in and out."

An incredible sensation washes over Captain Li. A rumble and a thrum down in her gut, in her marrow, in the lowest basest elements of her body. It is the vibration, the *sound*, of the very fabric of her being scrunching up and stretching out: the distance between the atoms of her body collapses, then expands. The cycle repeats again and again. For a moment she feels her fingertips and toes pulled away from her core, yanked by tidal forces. It feels like the lowest rumble of the biggest subwoofer ever built. It sounds like the deep voice of God whispering ASMR directly into her ear. It tingles, it thrills, and it leaves in its wake a subsonic tint of dread and anticipation.

She shivers hugely. "Gravity wave," she says. "Talk to me, Geode."

The Space-Time Geodesics Officer looks like she's just been hand-delivered a Nobel. "This is amazing!" she crows, fully aware that she and everyone else are about to die, but transported away from such temporal concerns by scientific rapture. "Can you feel that *growl*? We're experiencing high-frequency, high-amplitude gravity waves. Phaeton strikes. Axions decaying through the hull. Sterile neutrinos. It's all coming from a source at bearing, uh, zero four five mark zero three zero relative, range—range highly variable."

Another wave tears through *Yang Liwei*. Everything in the ship simultaneously compresses and stretches as the gravity wave deforms the space-time metric. "Is it the phantom?" Li demands, as her ship thrums subsonically. "Is that phantom ship emitting these waves?"

"I have no idea!" GEOD says, exultantly. "None of this makes any sense at all! Wow!"

Alice Li has the distinct sense that something ancient and malevolent is operating upon them: a trillion-fingered hand reaching in to caress the very atoms of their being, setting protons a-spin, strumming nerves like guitar strings. A tongue with ten billion slithering forks tasting the surface of their brains. The sense of imminent doom crescendos. She knows, absolutely and utterly, that what is about to happen to her and to her crew is far worse than death. The darkness knows them now. The thing that has come to kill humanity has their taste.

"INCO." She clings to her restraint harness as the ship growls through another wave. Her bones creak as they stretch. "Last report on the Traveler? Any sign of an intervention?"

"It was at Earth, Captain, and there were high-yield weapon discharges all over the signal. Nothing else."

"Understood." Well. She did not fly this far to look back and beg for salvation from an alien god. Pinned to the center of her sensorium is the blazing ledger of her crew's vote: *we go onward. We do not turn home. Our fate lies ahead of us, not behind.*

"Launch an antennae," she orders. "I want every probe and satellite we've got outside."

"Captain," INCO protests, "the vacuum's not signal-permissive—"

"We're still passing signals internally, aren't we? Use hardline! Run filament between the satellites! I want a transmitter sail out there and I want to broadcast."

Her flight crew stares. "Captain?" FIDO says. "Broadcast what?"

"A declaration of neutrality." Alice Li grits her teeth against another wave. It rattles her molars in her skull. "Whatever's out there, it came for the Traveler. We tell it we're not part of this war. We've seceded from human existence under the Traveler. We demand to be treated as a separate species, not party to baseline humanity's conflicts.

"And we pray there's something out there which cares about the difference."

8. COSMOGYRE IV [4500]

She remembers everything about the moment she is born.

She has gone outside *Yang Liwei* to die in starlight. She cannot bear to let anyone see her fear, or her awe at the scale of destruction, or her pity for the billions of souls dying in darkness back around Sol. She cannot be among the other crew as they cling to each other and whisper reassurances; not even with her mother. She cannot surrender her mystery.

So she kicks off the hull on fifty kilometers of tether.

But there's no starlight to die in. The darkness is absolute. Gravity waves tug on her line, pulling her back towards *Yang* and then hurling her away. In time she feels another vibration in the line. "Sister," the tether transmits. "I'm coming out to get you."

Brother, she thinks, you'll lose yourself trying to follow me.

Captain Li's voice breaks through the static, drawn out to a mumble and then compressed to a shriek. Spikes of hard radiation go through her words like bullets, spattering phonemes into eerie compression artifacts. *"This is the interstellar vessel* Yang Liwei *to the entity interacting with us. We are not involved in your dispute with the powers around this star. We are on a mission to begin a new life elsewhere. Our purpose is orthogonal to yours. We request your indifference..."*

Mara's tether trembles with Uldwyn's progress. She holds it in one hand and reaches out with the other, gripping the emptiness, feeling how the tides of broken space pull at her fingertips. She senses that the nothingness around her is not indifferent: that it is aware of all purposes, and that its own purpose encompasses them. It is infinitely hostile because it must be.

Then, as if the void around her has just spontaneously Big Banged, she sees light.

A point of pure white shines in the cosmic distance. Not just visible luminance—her suit decomposes the spectrum—but light in the radio bands, in microwave, keening ultraviolet, a spike of gamma, a total and all-embracing radiation. It sings. It chatters. It *speaks* in a voice older than suns. She feels that she could Fourier the voice for a century and never decompose it into its parts. It is awesome, and appalling, and piercingly true. Mara understands how those who die in radiation accidents must feel: a single flash of invisible power sears away all possible futures except for one. She feels that her soul itself has been ionized, blasted into a higher energy state.

The light pierces the darkness. Not like the sunrise, not like a wall or a flood, but a single crepuscular ray—a finger of radiance that reaches out through deepest night to touch her. It illuminates Mara, and Uldwyn, and *Yang Liwei*.

But it is not quite enough. It cannot vanquish the shadow.

Thus Mara finds herself drifting on the edge of the Light and the Darkness, on the dusk-and-dawn gradient between the two.

She feels a contest. A battle fought: an equilibrium reached: not a truce but an infinite limit, like an equation dividing by zero, a collision of two violent eternities. Mara queries *Yang Liwei* for telemetry and her sensorium fills with the terrified scream of gravitational instruments. She howls too, a feral sound, ecstatic and lost: a wolf baying at the stars. She knows what's happening. Too much power has gathered here. The universe is appalled by the paradox. Nothing that has glimpsed this collision of infinitudes can be allowed to escape. The cosmos must censor its embarrassment. It must sequester the anomaly.

The slope of warped space-time around them has become too steep, and now every path outward or forward bends back to the center where Light and Dark collide. The definition of 'future' has become synonymous with the definition of 'inward.' This why it is called an event horizon: for an object within the horizon, the path of all future things that can be done or seen leads inevitably down to the center. All events lead inward.

A singularity is forming around her. A *kugelblitz:* a black hole created by the concentration of raw energy.

"Mara!" Uldwyn shouts. "Mara, you're too far out!"

Mara thinks of her mother's face. She hears Osana say: I can't watch over you like a mother would. I have to make my own choices now.

She fires the *detach* command into the tether.

Gravity seizes her. She falls forward in space and time, into the future, into the mystery. *Yang Liwei* is behind her. Uldwyn is behind her. She wants to be the first....

9. ECSTASIATE I [2217]

to occur the unhappened world; to grip glass-hooped eternity in bloodslick hands, and snap it from its circle. Know her as the Flaw, the Isotropy, the spike that pierced eternal recurrence and made the wound of time. Tautologies end on her fingertips, in the crease between skin and nail. Name her AILILIA, Broth Captain. Begin with her this subcreation.

First. A mandala. Rings of rippled light. Pinpricks like stars: selected elements of a Lie group: the math-skeleton of this new place.

What is this? Where am I?

A sheet of paper, blank with static. Her hands flat upon the face. A plasma of quarks and electrons, so hot and bright that it is pitch black. The mean free path is too short for photons to travel. The fire is too thick for light.

She has been here forever. AILILIA. The end is the beginning is the end.

She folds the paper into Space and Time. Now that there is light she can read the paper, and she finds it is the Amrita Charter. "Sun is the cradle of life, but we cannot remain in the cradle forever." She was a seeker. The I of AILILIA, the arrow that points to new worlds: she sought new sun, new earth. Her mind passes across the words like a comb. Word becomes world, paper folds under nimble hands. The sting of a papercut: so God may yet be surprised.

From that cut her blood scatters through the void, and the isotropic universe nucleates around her droplets.

I am AILILIA, the guiding principle.

Bend the center. I am A L I S I L A, the arrow of time, sinuous but progressing.

I am A L I S I L I, one step forward, one element changed: this is how the world-clock ticks, by the letterwise permutation of secret names.

I am ALIS LI, the coalescence into entities, the compaction of drifting fire into sun and world.

I am Alis Li, the power that seeks new worlds. I have a crew. I had…a ship. I wanted to bring them to a place like—

(A paradise world: twin-ringed, impossible beauty, and a sky milk-bright with stars. She makes it real with a thought. And in that thought she falls herself, undoes her transient divinity, binds herself and all those after her into the law. The omniscient cannot explore. The omnipotent cannot struggle. She refuses that God-trap.)

—this.

This is how Alice Li awakens.

10. ECSTASIATE II [2676]

She was nothingness. If she existed before then she existed only as possibility stretched across the aether. Once there might have been a body that was an anticipation of the body not yet formed, and a soul that was an anticipation of the soul not yet encrypted, but they were not yet real.

Then the universe began, and she was free to be born.

First there is a mandala, and upon the rings of that mandala there are star-bright gems.

M A R A R A M the closed symmetry, secret within itself: and she cuts it off center so that it is imperfect, open at one end, not cycling back to its own beginning but subliming away into future possibility. M A R A the permutation of one relationship into another, MA become RA, RA become what may yet come. Two points suggest a line.

And with that amputation, around that scar, she incarnates. Awakens with a gasp. Cold stone under her shoulders and back: and a face above her, radiant. "Mara?" the face says.

"What am I?" Mara whispers.

"The second," the woman says. "I'm Alis. I think you were Mara…"

The sky behind Alis blooms with stars, a haze of light like sun through mist, richer than a galactic core. And across that night sky arches the impossible twin shape of a double planetary ring. Mara gapes in wonder. "I remember," she says. "I was on the tether—"

But the sudden need to keep this memory secret shuts her mouth. "We're on a world," she says, instead. "How long have you been alone?"

"Forever, I think. Come." She draws Mara to her feet. "I want to show you what I've found."

It is a world that grows, a world that thrives. The stone is rich with veins of platinum, and Mara tastes tingling inclusions of transuranic elements in a fingertip of earth. Silver rivers flow in fractal deltas to lakes as still and bright as coolant pools. Acres of forests all woven at the root into a single tree. There is life of such variety and energy that each new crawling thing they see must be its own species. Or species do not mean anything at all here, and all that lives may intermingle.

Jutting from the horizon they find a titanic metal spear. The head of the spear is a metal dish, kilometers across, buried in bedrock.

"I don't know what this is," Alis says. "I only know that it's mine."

They pass inside.

"There should be others," Mara says, afterwards. "There was room for others. Thousands of others. Where are they?"

"They're in the same place you came from. We have to make them real." Li stares at Mara, and coruscations of white fire map the tiny lines and furrows of her skin. Her bright eyes narrow. "Why were you the second? Why you in particular?"

"I don't know," Mara lies. It is the first lie ever told, the first secret kept.

11. ECSTASIATE III [3851]

Two became four, and the four called out, and so the four became eight. In this manner, conjured forth by their doubling, the sleepers did awaken. In time the awoken spilled across the face of the world, and their number was forty thousand and eight hundred and ninety one. They drank of the sweet rain, and they ate of the fruit of the forest, and the starlight pooled as clear oil on their skin. First of their tongues was Speech, and the first of their hunting weapons was the bow.

Now the awoken called out for a name to distinguish World from Unworld. The eight hundred and ninety one said to the forty thousand, "Let this world be named Tributary, for we dream of a great river from which we have parted." But the forty thousand were troubled, and they asked to know their antecedent, the place from which they came. "We did not awaken from the sleep that we entered," said the forty thousand. "In our rest we passed through some terminus and our atavism was severed from us. How did it happen thus?"

So a council was called at the place where the rivers met to determine the nature and purpose of existence. Here was undertaken the first census, which counted thirty thousand one hundred and eleven women, ten thousand two hundred and ninety five men, and four hundred and eighty five otherwise. A fear arose among the awoken that the men and otherwise would be lost.

Alis Li spoke first in council, but at the urging of Uldren, many sought out Mara for secret conclave. Among these were Kelda Wadj who would be the Allteacher, and Sila who would be mother of Esila.

Sayeth Alis, "We were granted this world by a covenant with high powers, and in that covenant we yielded our claim to our history. We abandoned what came before, but in doing so, we cast off all our debts. Look forward! Let us explore this infant cosmos, and revel in its glories!"

Against her spoke Owome An, who was of the forty thousand. "We are alien here," said Owome. "We must climb up our worldline, back to the place from which we came. I call for a vote."

Sayeth Mara, in secret, "I think that we came here as safe harbor, and we cannot forever remain. I remember the danger was appalling. I remember we were born in death. I think that we must gather ourselves carefully, until the time is right."

From this council there arose eight verdicts and a ninth.

First, that the people were Awoken, and they were immortal.

Second, that this world was Tributary of another, but that it was forbidden to seek any way to rejoin the mother stream. For this reason it would be called Distributary, for that was the proper name for a river which branches from the mother and does not return.

Third, that the Awoken should multiply in wombs of flesh and machine, but only after the most careful forecast of population and ecology, and only under the supervision of those who knew the good technology; for each new child would be immortal.

Fourth, that those wise in the good technology should be heralded and heeded, so that the eu-technology could be preserved. They would be eutechs.

Fifth, that the women should hold care and protection of the men and the others until more could be born.

Sixth, that the purpose of the Awoken should be to know and love the cosmos.

Seventh, that the Awoken were created out of covenant with Light and Darkness, but the covenant was complete, and no further debt would ever be called, except the duty of the Second Verdict to remain Distributary.

Eighth, that the Awoken were whole in themselves, and that they existed in balance.

Ninth, that there would be no vote, but instead Alis Li would be recognized as Queen. Her first pronunciation was that there would be no secrets among Awoken.

For Alis knew of the quiet council around Mara, and although she was neither jealous nor afraid, she remembered it carefully as a spark which might catch.

12. FIDEICIDE I [2127]

In those days there was a great birth of adventure among the Awoken. Hunters and pioneers sought the shape of the world, sailors charted the skein of rivers and the perimeter of seas, and astronomers plotted the motion of the crowded heavens. Over this age ruled Queen Alis Li, whose work was the creation of agriculture and the preservation of the eutechnology which she deciphered from the Shipspire.

But there remained in the forests many tribes of huntresses who preferred their lightfooted freedom-from-comfort-and-duty to the painstaking surplus of the city. Among these tribes Mara lived with her brother whose name had returned as Uldren and with Osana their mother. It is said that Osana lived as a negotiator, and that her son brought her news from other tribes, for he was a scout and hunter of renown. But Mara dwelt alone on a mountaintop.

In the tribes of the forests and the sea there was the belief that the Awoken had been made out of a friction between contesting forces, and that one day this conflict would need to be resolved. These were the Eccaleists who preached that Awoken owed a debt to the cosmos.

But in the cities they lived by the Seventh Verdict under their Queen, and they said that the Awoken had been created by cosmic gift and carried neither responsibility nor eschaton. These were the Sanguine, who preached that the Awoken were as stable as an atom of carbon.

Now there arose among the Eccaleists a woman out of the eight hundred and ninety one who called herself the Diasyrm. She went into the cities, calling out, "I accuse the Queen of deicide!" And when she was questioned she spoke of a foundational crime.

"Alis Li was the first to awaken in this world," the Diasyrm preached. "She set the terms of our existence. We could have been gods free of want or suffering. But Alis Li chose our mortal form. Our Queen is complicit in all the pain we experience! The Queen murdered all our unborn godheads!"

At the thought that the Queen Without Secrets had kept this most appalling secret to herself, the Sanguine cityfolk were deeply troubled. Thus began the Theodicy War.

13. FIDEICIDE II [3666]

"It wasn't supposed to be like this," Alis Li whispers, as, far down below the Shipspire, the funeral barges on the Lake of Leaves burst up into magnesium-white fire. The voices of the paladins rise on summer wind, first choral, then the single keening strains of grief-paeans sung by lovers and close friends. They are singing their lost comrades into death. One of the 891 fell today, shot down by a matter laser, a coherent boson weapon: there was almost nothing left to burn. Matter lasers are the kind of appalling maltech weapon Alis thought she'd locked up in the Shipspire's vaults. She'd armed a few of her paladins with them, just a few, women she couldn't bear to lose…

The thought that one might have defected to the Diasyrm breaks her heart.

"It wasn't supposed to go this way," Alis repeats. She has not had a confidante in nigh on fifty years: there is no one to whom she can show any doubt. "I promise you it wasn't."

"I know," Mara says. The eutechs found her and plucked her from her mountaintop with one of the Shipspire's VTOL aircraft, which Alis had, until the war, only ever used as an ambulance.

"The mission was to carry on the human journey in a new world." Alis paces the wooden deck that clings to the Shipspire airlock, nearly a kilometer above the lake. "To build a better society, on the principles of equality, knowledge, and peace. I have the charter, Mara. It remembers what I cannot. We were never meant to give up our bodies, or shine like stars, or—or—" She groans in frustration and clutches the railing. "Or whatever it is that the Diasyrm thinks I denied them."

"She thinks you denied them even the capability to imagine godhood."

Alis looks sharply back at the other woman. "Did you start this, Mara?"

"Nothing has one beginning," Mara says.

"Did she come to you on your mountaintop and ask you what I did? Did you answer her? Is that why she's so convinced I," she swallows against the bitter taste of her enemy's words, "enslaved her in mere humanity?"

"I didn't have to tell her." Mara's white hair stirs in the hot wind. A herd of black horses crosses the northern horizon, all born of Shipspire's wombs: chased by a long-legged huntress and her collie. "You don't keep enough secrets, your Majesty. The Diasyrm might have opened any one of your texts and read the story you tell. *We were born when a great ship fell into a pearl of shattered space. I awoke first, and in my awakening I collapsed the potential of the void into a form I understood…* Who can read that truth and not hear arrogance?"

Alis thought Mara might say that. Alis also thought Mara might try to push her off the balcony, but she now knows that was a petty fear. Mara is not the Diasyrm: Mara knows the unthinkable value of even a single Awoken life.

"Why do you love lies so much?" she asks Mara.

"Not lies." The pale radiance of Mara's eyes; the flush of violet stain around them. "Secrets. Even if everyone shared a single truth, all our minds would produce different versions of the truth. We speak these subtruths, and like flowers of different seed the subtruths compete for the light of our attention. In time only the fiercest and most provocative strains remain. They are not always the truest. Better to keep secrets, your Majesty. Better to tend a great mystery, and so starve the flowers before they can grow. That is how I would be Queen."

Down below the Lake of Leaves shimmers in the crater carved by Shipspire's mushroom prow. One by one the funeral boats are going out.

"I want to end this war," Alis Li tells the second Awoken. "I want to negotiate a peace. I need your mother's help. What would you ask in exchange?"

Mara smiles graciously, and bows her head. "Nothing but a future boon."

14. FIDEICIDE III [2768]

To end a world with a shot, or pin eternity on a blade; to see your sisters lost to rot, and their undone works decayed. The death of an immortal wastes the infinite potential of all they might become. And an immortal's grief and murder-guilt, left untended, will never fade. Thus it became known to those who fought in the Theodicy War that they had committed an incomparable evil. But they could not confront their own responsibility. So they rose up in wrath against those who had given them cause, whether by caging them in flesh bodies or by drawing blood over grievance. The war continued by spear and bow, by knife and scalpel, by old machine and new invention. Ever did the Diasyrm's faithful call for the unawaring of Queen Alis Li.

Now there entered into the Diasyrm's camp Osana, mother of Mara, famed for her skill in negotiating contested land. She had come with her son Uldren, who could win a place in any camp for his beauty and for the regal crow-eagle that alighted on his shoulder.

"I come from Mara," said Osana, "whose heart has frozen in her chest. If you will end the killing she will tell you any secret that you desire."

For his part Uldren went among the Diasyrm's warriors and spread ill tidings of Mara's knowledge, saying, "Mara remembers how the Queen led us here out of chaos, and saved us from the twin blindness of darkness and light. Mara knows what the Queen keeps secret. Mara has seen the strife in our souls, the clash from which we were made. We could not ever have been gods with this flaw in us! Rather we were made from this schism. For as all life is born from energy gradient, as life in the World Before was born from the gradient between hot proton-rich ventwater and cold seawater, we were born of the shadowline at the edge of Light and Dark. We are tremors in that fault. Forever will that schism lead us."

Hearing this new heresy the Eccaleists were seized with rapture, and scattered to the points of the compass, telling all they met "We are the yield of a mighty engine! We could never have been gods! Like diamonds we were crushed into being. Like diamonds we hold flaws."

Meanwhile Osana spoke to the Diasyrm, who was also heartsick from the killing, and who longed to withdraw from the world and seek transcendence within. "There is no weregild for the murder of an immortal," Osana counseled her. "You must become a teacher or a midwife, and devote yourself to the enrichment of new lives."

But the Diasyrm craved secret knowledge, and she sought Mara upon the mountaintop. Here she vanished. If she was ever known again it was not by the name Diasyrm.

When there was peace Queen Li ruled the Awoken for a time. But the guilt of the war lay heavy upon her, and after an age of peace and progress she abdicated to a new Queen.

15. HERESIOLOGY [4990]

A woman lives alone on the forest hills above the Feather Barrens. North of her, in a chaos of ravines and clear but fiercely radioactive streams, the hills surrender to high imperial mountains engaged in brutal seismic warfare, for Distributary is a young world and has not settled its grudges. To the south are the dry lands where the birds of the forest, especially the parrots, go to die. She lives here because one day she will no longer be immortal, and she wants to observe the dignity of death.

Up these hills come a man and his mother. The man moves with practiced wariness. But his mother is tired of walking, so she sits down on a giant melon and bellows "MARAAA!"

A fountain of startled birds shoots up into the dawnlight. Not far away, the woman looks up from the broken body of a juvenile grey parrot and softly says "Mom?"

That night over the fire, after Mara and Osana talk around the oddness of long separation, Mara, tending the pheasants on their spits, says, "Brother, your eagle killed a parrot today."

"He had to hunt," Uldren says, carefully. "You won't forbid him his last pleasures, will you?"

"You've brought him here to die?" Mara wants to leap up and hug her brother, out of pity and respect. Many of his raptors have died before this one, but Uldren has always been grief-stricken and furious at the waste. Now he's accepted what must happen; he has given his bird the respect of choosing its own place and time to pass.

"I have," Uldren says, looking away. Her pride and respect make him a little verklempt. "And mother decided she would come along."

A shear force as powerful as tectonics has divided Mara's heart. She wants to sit down with her mother and ask her everything; but she is afraid of Osana's insight. "What brings you to my little camp, mother?"

"Lies," Osana says. "Lies and secrets. And the girl who didn't want to be my daughter, who doesn't know the difference between them."

"I know the difference between a girl and a daughter," Mara says, purposefully misunderstanding. The drip pan sizzles beneath golden meat. Her stomach growls. "Your daughter picks up your baton at the end of the race, and goes on living the life you've taught her. You wouldn't want that, mother. Because then I'd be all your fault."

"That's true," Osana sighs. "But you know what I meant."

Uldren looks between the two of them, frowning. "Mom, what's this?"

"It's your sister about to admit she's behind it all. Aren't you, Mara?"

She unimpales the pheasants from the spits and neatly licks hot grease off her hands. If she spoke, she might scream in terror. What does that mean, behind it all? Does Osana know?

"The Eccaleists are her creation," her mother tells her brother. "The Diasyrm was her pawn. She allowed the Theodicy War because she was afraid that we'd be too comfortable here, and also so that Queen Alis would need her help politically. Mara couldn't afford to be the most radical dissident. She had to seem moderate for her beliefs to thrive. Isn't that right, Mara?"

Mara puts a hand into the warm soil to keep herself from slumping in relief. Mother doesn't know it all. "Shall I carve your portions?" she asks, holding the fractal knife politely blade-down.

Uldren has that look. He knows Mara never answers his questions directly: by evading Osana's, it's as if she's saying that the question is really Uldren's to ask. "Looks delicious. But Mother does make me curious. Why have you always lived away from the rest of us, Mara? The mountaintop I understood. You had a brand new night sky to chart. But why now? Why go into the woods like a…a hermit? A heretic?"

For the same reason she lived on the hull. For the same reason she can never allow Uldren to really reach her. There is power in remove, and also safety from the belittling politics of temporal power, which reveal the mighty as unforgivably ordinary and petty. The Awoken have a Queen because a Queen can be a mystery.

"I remember the day I was born," she says. "Do you, brother?"

He flinches from her eyes. He remembers *Yang Liwei* and the tether into darkness. He remembers how gravity stretched them into agonized ribbons of flesh. He remembers the truth not even Alis Li may be allowed to know: Mara sees the agonizing moment, the cyclic revelation, when he thinks of her crime, allows it to pierce him like a spit, and buries it deep again.

Osana takes her portion of pheasant meat and rolls it in the bowl of sweet cooked nuts her daughter has prepared. The stars are coming out over the mountains, and the forest birds sing. "This place is good," she says. "This world. Whatever you remember of our lives before, Mara…I know they cannot have been this good."

"No," Mara says. "But you were both with me. And I hope you always will be."

"Always," her brother promises.

"Eat well." Mara claps her hands and stands. "Tomorrow we journey."

"Where?" her mother asks.

"I have star charts to share." And heresies to tend to. And a new eagle-crow to find for her bereft brother.

16. IMPONENT I [2747]

In later days the power of the Queen waned, and the Distributary was ruled by scholars who sent their knights on mad quests to test the consistence of reality. These were the Gensym Scribes, who traced their origin to Kelda Wadj the Allteacher, but who were in fact descendants of a band of roving storytellers who traveled across the immense salt glades in a hollering convoy of airboats. Here was their praise of the world:

It is sweet-watered and there are no poisons upon it. The temper of the climate is even. Great broad-pawed cats stalk the shallow glades, and brilliant blue flamingos promenade upon the flats. The air is thick and warm, suited for flight, and the wind tastes of forest. No dawn has ever been as glorious as the salt glade dawn, and no dusk has ever moved women to weep as deeply as sunset in the Chriseiads. Corsairs sport upon the open seas, and where they waylay freighters rather than each other, they give rumor and assistance to their prey in proportion to the quality of the chase. Beloved are the stories of young lads and lasses who leap across to the corsair ship for a life of adventure! Beloved also are the terraced farms of the Andalayas, mountains so mighty and so dense with radioactives that they subside year by year into the crust. Most beloved are the fissioneers, who vaulted us to power on a world without petrochemicals. May they forgive the many stories of horror we have told in their memory. May they in particular forgive the lurid stories of the molten lead reactor, and the twelve who were impaled to the ceiling by their control rods, and the Core That Stalked.

It is the Sanguine Truth that we were granted this world by the unconditional mercy of the powers, and that we will never again know fear.

But the Scribes also recorded their frustration with Mara and Uldren, who alone out of the Eight Hundred and Ninety One were said to have seen creation from outside. These two wandered the land gathering lore of portents and prophecies. And all the Eccaleists who remained from ancient days whispered that soon the day of reckoning would be known, the day when the Awoken would be called to repay their debt.

Now in the court of one of the Scribes there appeared a woman of stellar height and furious wrath, armed with a bow that could only be strung if she twined it around her body and used her whole mass to bend it. "I am Sjur Eido," said the woman, "and I accuse Mara of the ancient murder of my lady the Diasyrm. In my saddle I have a weapon with only one death remaining in it. Take me to Mara and I will use it on her."

The Scribes consulted, and said to each other that this foul murder might prevent another Theodicy War. So they gave Sjur Eido all their knowledge to hunt Mara.

17. IMPONENT II [3528]

Carefully the people of Distributary grew in number. Joyously and constantly they grew in quality. Those who do not die are as malleable and passionate as the young, as tempered and constant as the mature, and as wise and humble as the best of the old.

But as ever the Awoken were troubled by death. It was easy to imagine a world older and harsher than Distributary, a world crowded with competitors where the slow-changing and lushly alive Awoken would be helpless beside austere mayfly-quick breeders who adapted with every swift generation.

Why had the Awoken been spared mortality? Were they, as the Sanguine preached, rewarded for their bravery and fidelity in a past existence? Or were the Eccaleists right? Could all the gifts of Distributary, all the milk-bright stars above, all the years of Awoken life, be a form of cowardice? Was there an unfought battle down in the center of the Awoken soul? A duty yet to be discharged?

Queen Nguya Pin restored the monarchy to prominence over the Gensym Scribes. This she accomplished after a fateful visit, upon the day of the summer solstice, by a hooded and masked woman who some whispered was Mara Sov and others the long-vanished Diasyrm. For nine and ninety years (a rhetorical figure meaning a long time) the Queen had been an authority only in the arts and matters spiritual. But Queen Nguya Pin declared that she was now an avowed Eccaleist, and that the Queen would lead the quest to identify whatever debt the Awoken owed to the cosmos. It was time to pursue a dream beloved to all Awoken: the conquest of space, and the assessment of the true shape and age of their universe.

The ancient court of the Queen gave the Gensym Scribes a place to lay down their pride and act as equals. Soon the greatest engineers in the world assembled in the Queen's court, and whatever wealth and resources they required flowed freely. Great cataracts of men and women spilled around the palace, screaming of ramjets and apoapses deep into the night, then awakening to pots of thick black coffee to mumble about metric tensors and cosmic microwave anisotropy.

Into this feast of ideas came Sjur Eido, searching for the woman who had turned Queen Pin to Eccaleism. Sjur smoldered with an ancient fury, for another thing that the immortal may nurture is everlasting vendetta.

Sjur Eido deduced who among the Queen's court must be a disguised Mara Sov. She followed the hooded figure to her laboratory, and watched Mara go to work soldering a makeshift bolometer to search for signs of primordial gravity waves. Sjur Eido's fury and grief whetted themselves against Mara's thoughtless grace and ancient beauty, until at last her heart unseamed itself and spilled its hot blood in a shout. "Mara Sov!" she cried, throwing down her maltech matter laser between them. "I cannot live while you live, but I cannot bear to kill you. I challenge you to a duel to the agony. I will fight your most beloved companion to the death, and leave you forever maimed; or else die in the attempt."

Mara could not refuse this challenge. She summoned Uldren, and with a ruthlessness that no longer frightened her to wield, she told Uldren that he would stand for her in battle to the death against Sjur Eido.

"We cannot put it all upon a single fight," Uldren said to the ancient vendetta-bearer. "Too much would be left to chance. Such an old grudge deserves to be tested well. I propose we fight with blade, with rifle, and with fifth-generation air superiority fighters."

Sjur Eido accepted these terms.

18. IMPONENT III [3497]

Now it came to pass that Esila daughter of Sila recognized the scent of Sjur Eido, for smell lies deepest in memory. Esila spoke to Queen Nguya Pin about the presence of an ancient hero in her court. While Queen Pin pondered how to honor this visitor, and simmered over the insult given by Sjur's unannounced presence, a spy brought word of Sjur Eido's intentions to the Gensym Scribes.

The many Scribes were troubled by this news, for they had given Sjur Eido license to hunt and kill Mara Sov. If Sjur Eido murdered a guest of the Queen under the Scribes' remit, it would mean war and the end of the great Awoken push for space. Historians were called to the court with bouquets of sweet flowers and grant money to speak of Sjur Eido. "She was one of Queen Alis Li's Paladins, but she was an Eccaleist, who believed that we would one day be called to repay the gift of our awakening."

"Would she defy the Queen's protection and murder a guest of the court?" the Scribes asked.

"Oh, absolutely," the historians said, laughing. "She was a terror."

The Scribes began preparations to flee the Queen's court, as they foresaw Sjur Eido's victory would be blamed upon them. Sensing uncertainty, many vital contractors and suppliers withdrew from the space program. The Queen denounced the Gensym Scribes as faithless and selfish, and her Eccaleist followers bristled in rage against the Sanguine majority who had scuttled their dream of flight. Household turned against household, sister against brother, wife against wife. The whole world clenched her fists.

Meanwhile Sjur Eido and Uldren met each other on a net of woven lianas over a pool of heavy water. The light of the Queen's reactors shimmered beneath them as they took their places. Uldren wore a white chestpiece of ceramic armor over a suit of black tasseled silk, and he wielded a long fractal knife whose cutting edge was nearly three times as long as the blade. Sjur Eido fought in the contoured blue-grey pressure armor of a Paladin with the Star of Eight Edicts blazoned on her chest.

Before they began, Sjur Eido tore away the sheer curtain over the gardener's nook and looked in on Mara Sov. "Are you afraid?" she whispered, half in hatred, half in admiration, all in awe. "Do you sweat? Does your breath come short?"

Mara pressed her hand to Sjur's faceplate and left no stain. She held Sjur's gauntlet to her heart so Sjur could feel her steady pulse and even breath. "You don't care about him?" Sjur pressed her. "It would mean nothing if I maimed him?"

"You ask the right questions," Mara said, "but of the wrong sibling."

Then Sjur understood that she fought a man who would always express his love through loss and ordeal.

She bowed to Uldren and drew her knife. Uldren bowed in mocking reply. They fought across the web of lianas in a slow spiral, creeping like spiders, waiting for the motion of the web beneath them to signal an instant of vulnerability. Then the pounce, the clash, the blur of knives: Sjur Eido's straightforward prisonyard jabs against Uldren's whirling deceptive theater. All of knife fighting is in the seizure and surrender of space: neither would surrender to the close, the clinch, the berserk adrenaline-sick exchange of thrusts that would leave both dead.

Uldren began to cut away key lianas to throw Sjur Eido's footing, and Sjur Eido countered by charging him to keep him off balance. At last they fell together into the coolant pond. The fight was a draw: but it was only the first of three.

19. IMPONENT IV [3371]

Next the fallen Paladin and the hunter chose long guns and went out into the monsoon jungle to stalk each other. Sjur Eido selected a Tigerspite in 11x90mm with five-round flock guidance and an inertial sump. Uldren chose a silent needle carbine with a conesnail payload. For six weeks they stalked each other as the political situation grew more dire. He was the better hunter, stealthier in motion and at ease in the wilderness. But Sjur Eido was the better soldier: she had no respect for the systems of the jungle, and she knew how to use that to her advantage. She drove the animals into a frenzy with violence and disruption of habitat. Parrots and crows warned each other of Uldren's stealthy hides, and jealous predators forced him off his carefully scouted trails. Sjur Eido caught him with his back against a rift lake, and shot him as he tried to cross the lakebed. The wound was not mortal, for the water ruined the terminal ballistics: but she had won the match.

"Your life is at stake," Mara warned her brother. "Lose this final match, and you will—"

"Am I simple?" he snarled at her. The wound pained him terribly, but he would not risk more than a little analgesic. "Leave me my work, sister, or you leave me nothing at all."

Now they would meet in air superiority fighters over the Andalayas. Charges under their seats would detonate if either of them left the engagement area. Because of the small combat zone, Sjur Eido chose a nimble Ermine tactical fighter and a payload of all-aspect heatseeking missiles.

"Where will we receive these aircraft?" Uldren demanded. "How can I trust the equipment?"

Sjur Eido told him that one of the Gensym Scribes would provide the aircraft and requested weapons from her personal deterrent stockpile. "Very well," Uldren sniffed. "And we will have access to all the weapons these airframes can equip?"

"Of course," Sjur said. "Those we cannot obtain can be replaced by training simulators." She was certain Uldren's wound would cripple him.

"Then I will fly a Dart," Uldren said. The ancient interceptor had awful fire control, dismal maneuverability, and primitive weapons.

"A Dart?" Sjur jeered. "Will you fly with its original weapons, too? You think you can beat me with rockets and a gun?"

"I do," Uldren purred. "You accept those terms?" She did.

The two duelists took to the skies on a bright winter morning. After a fuel check, a telemetry squawk, and a terrain snapshot, they turned in towards each other from a hundred kilometers apart. Sjur Eido descended for the terrain, knowing

Uldren's radar could barely separate her from the clutter. Uldren came straight on.

At eighty kilometers of separation, Uldren called across the radio "Fox three. Kill. Engagement over." Sjur sneered at the bluff and prepared to climb into a snap attack—when the KILLED alert flashed on her Ermine's training panel. She had forgotten that the Dart's intercept loadout, when it had last served seventy years ago, included an unguided air-to-air nuclear rocket. Uldren had simulation-killed her and everything within several klicks.

On the tarmac, Sjur Eido threw off her helmet and parachute and knelt before Mara Sov. "My lady," she said, "as I have fought your brother to a tie, I leave my fate in your hands. Be more kind to me than you were to my lady the Diasyrm."

"Rise, Sjur Eido," said Mara. "Let us take the stars together."

20. IMPONENT V [3765]

The subsonic roar of the solid rocket boosters crosses the threshold from noise into motion. To hear it is to feel it, and to feel it is to remember that you are a sack of fluids and gels much more than you are a solid entity. Membranes and gradients, solutes and films: a body is a mingled thing. Mara thinks of this as she watches the launch vehicle discard its boosters and climb away through the clouds. The Awoken could have been angels. Instead they are flesh.

"That's that." Queen Nguya Pin rises from her portable throne, unfolding two heads taller than Mara. "Choose your replacement. My work is done, and I will stomach no more."

Mara smiles at her. "Is a Queen's work ever done?"

"Oh, don't insult me," Queen Pin clucks. She brushes windblown pollen from her trousers: today's launches have blasted the spring trees with hot wind. "You used me to do your work, politically and scientifically. You used me to bundle up the Scribes in a neat little scroll for your disposal. I went along with it for the sake of the monarchy, Mara, not because I'm a fool. I don't know what you want, or why you're so bent on keeping the Awoken uneasy and dissatisfied. I don't know how you manipulate the acclamations. But when I abdicate I am going to find Alis Li, wherever she's gone, and ask her all my questions about you. I'm very interested to know the answers."

"You've been a wonderful queen," Mara says. "No one will ever replace you." Although she is thinking of Devna Tel, who was never one of the Scribes, and whose coronation would make a wonderful rebuke to the Scribes' remaining ambitions.

Sjur Eido meets her by the ship. "We'll need a new queen," Mara tells her, leaping up the side of the ramp. "Word on the satellite?"

"Still burning for the Lagrange point. What have you done to Nguya?"

"Given her too much perspective, I'm afraid." Just as this observatory satellite should help the Awoken see things from Mara's point of view. She smiles as she helps her bodyguard up the ramp, Sjur indulgently pretending that she needs Mara's hand. "Uldren should be on the ground in Kamarina by now. We'll have a go-ahead on that interferometer buyout when he's done."

There are new stars in the sky. Mara put them there. Huge distributed-array telescopes orbit Distributary's cool sun; gravity wave sensors and cold primordial neutrino detectors spider the crust. Out of shell corporations and seed investments she has opened her world as an enormous eye and focused it heavenward. Sjur Eido was her smiling public avatar these past decades, while her brother handled enforcement. The days of covert speed chess in the Queen's court are over: Sjur Eido's open endorsement made Mara the face of Eccaleism, and armed Mara with blackmail over all the Gensym Scribes still in power.

Yet she has never been so lonely or so worried for the future. Mother has told her that she, Mara, uses her power over Uldren too freely: that she must learn to stop, or her mother will no longer be her friend.

"Mara?" Sjur says, catching some flickering expression. Knowing Mara well, she immediately changes tack away from comfort. "What do you think we'll find with the satellite?"

"Proof that it's time for us to go," Mara says. "Proof of what I've known since the beginning."

Sjur frowns in thought. She doesn't remember much from before her awakening: few of the 891 do. But enough to trouble her. "Time for us to go…"

The ship's turbines keen up to speed and then settle into whisper-quiet cruise. Sjur reaches to strap herself in across from Mara. Impulsively, hard-faced, denying she needs what she is asking for, Mara scoots aside to make room on her bench. Sjur raises an eyebrow at her.

"Don't say anything," Mara warns her. "Not a word." And so they pass the flight in silence, but not alone.

21. KATABASIS [4063]

Mara looks into the camera and lets the fire in her eyes speak.

They are waiting on her, the Distributary's millions, her Awoken people. She has stoked their curiosity with thirty years of painstaking analysis. When they look up at the night sky they see the stars of her observatories among the crowded bands of habitats, the spindly orbital factories, towering elevator counterweights, the burning roads of matter streams.

"Let me tell you of our world," she says.

There are the facts of tectonics and atmosphere, of water and climate: the parameters of the sun that feeds them. "No infants died last year. No child went unfed. No youth came of age illiterate, no one suffered illness who might have been treated. We have long surpassed the eutech gathered from Shipspire; yet we have grown carefully and cleanly. We have eluded pollution, eradicated plague, and chosen peace. No maltech weapon has been discharged in centuries. Our atomic weapons were dismantled before they could ever be used. We are our own triumph."

She has elected not to use graphics or theater. She would rather they remember her face.

"You know yourselves," she says. "Let me tell you of your cosmos. We live in a spatially infinite, isotropic universe 12.1 billion years old. Its metallicity is ideal for life, and for the spread of technological civilizations. In time the distance between all points in the universe will contract to zero, and the cosmos will collapse into a singularity, to be reborn in fire. There will be no end to eternity here."

She pauses. She waits. The whole world is out there, begging for the answer to the question.

"Our world is a gift. And we must refuse it."

They are Awoken. They love secrets. They will wait for her to explain.

"We have detected a pattern that was imprinted into our universe by its ancestor: a fingerprint of the initial conditions into which existence was born. From this information we have confirmed the most primordial of Awoken myths. Our universe is a subset of another. We live within a singularity, a knot in space-time, that orbits a star in another world.

"Conventional relativity would suggest that time outside an event horizon passes quickly compared to a clock within: but our universe has a peculiar relationship with its mother. Thousands of years have passed for us on Distributary. Outside? Centuries, at most. We are a swift eddy in a slow river.

"These ideas may not surprise you, after centuries of theorizing and philosophy.

But we have decrypted new data from the cosmic microwave and neutrino background signals. We have discovered voices…the voices of distress calls. They tell a story of bravery, of war, and of desperate loss.

"We were not always immortal. We did not earn this utopia by covenant with any cosmic power, or by attaining an enlightened moral condition. We are refugees. We fled from an apocalyptic clash between our ancestors' civilization and an invading power." She lowers her eyes. "The signals we have retrieved tell us that our ancestors were on the edge of defeat. Perhaps extinction."

"It is time that we accept our debt. Distributary is a refuge, not a birthright. A base to rebuild our strength, not a garden to tend. I ask you, Awoken, to join me in the hardest and most worthy task a people has ever faced. We must leave our heaven, return to the world of our ancestors, and take up the works they abandoned. If some of them survive, we must offer aid. If they have enemies, we must share our strength. We must go back to the war we fled and face our enemies there."

She lets them dangle a moment before she drives it home. "We have also determined that our birthright, our immortality, is tied to the fundamental traits of this universe. Once we leave, we will begin to age again. In time we will all die.

"Will you join me, Awoken? Will you answer my call? All I offer you is hardship and death. All I ask is everything you can offer. But you will see an older starlight. You will walk in a deeper dark than this world has ever known."

22. NIGH I [3909]

"You're the devil," Alis Li whispers. "I remember, in one of the old tongues, Mara means death…"

An hour before. Mara's ship touches down a polite two kilometers from the Pearl Groves, and she looks out across mazes of channel and tidal pond to the compounds of ancient silver-white stone beyond. Two-ton oysters glitter in the shallows, their shells jeweled with mineral inclusions. Seabirds peck and fret along narrow white beaches. Mara lifts up her black formal skirts and begins her long walk into Alis Li's retreat, the sanctuary of former queens.

"Mara," Uldren whispers, through her throat mic. "Don't do this. Take Sjur with you, at least."

But she has to do this, or she'll never be able to face herself again.

The sun batters at her. She hides under a parasol but heat gathers in the folds of her garment, in the soles of her shoes. When she squints against the glare she thinks she can see the shining grains of her fleet in orbit: the Hulls, built under eutech supervision to the specifications of radically post-conscious AI, that will one day fly between worlds. It is far too late to stop the project now. Far, far too late for second thoughts: exactly twelve point one billion years too late, really. For Mara in particular.

Mara kicks the sand and trudges on.

She's in a foul mood when she reaches the old Queen's house, but the sight of Alis Li sitting on the porch with a battered tea service makes her smile. "Thank you for seeing me," Mara says.

"Thank you for coming. I was afraid you'd leave the universe without saying goodbye." Alis pours her a cup of cool blackberry tea. "Have a seat. How's Queen Tel?"

"She has declined to endorse my expedition," Mara admits, tucking her feet beneath her on the wide wooden deck chair. The tea is too sweet, but so blissfully cool. "I'm sure you understand her reasons."

"You mean she's declined to endorse the sudden violent severance of tens of thousands of threads from the tapestry of our society? How surprising." Alis looks Mara over, critically, then sits back to sigh. "A Scribe once told me that the definition of a utopia is a place where every single person's happiness is necessary to everyone else. You're going to make a lot of unhappy people, Mara. You'll make the lives of everyone in the world tangibly worse. Not just those you've lured to certain death, but those who will grieve their departure, and all those who will come to grief for lack of labor and knowledge you took with you."

"My people volunteered."

"Your mother told me," Alis says, "that it is one thing for you to have a particular power over people, but another thing entirely to deny that you are using it."

"You once told me," Mara counters, "that I had to consider the symbol people made out of me, and that if it were good, then I had to be that symbol for them. I had to perform as they required. I have done so. I have been the best thing I can think to be."

"Is this the best thing you could think to be?" Alis says, with very practiced neutrality.

Mara drinks her tea in delicate silence.

The old Queen sets her cup down hard enough to chip. Mara jumps in quiet shock: the tea service is an heirloom from Shipspire. Her face hardens with the power of ancient command. "Mara. I'm at least as clever as you. Do me the credit of acknowledging it."

"I have worked for many hundreds of years to arrange this outcome," Mara says, forthrightly, but without the courage to look Alis Li right in the eyes. "I have nurtured and tended the Eccaleist belief so that there will always be Awoken who feel uncomfortable in paradise. Guilty for the gift of existence in Distributary. People who'll come with me."

"I know." Alis lays a hand on Mara's, and for a moment the touch almost makes Mara sigh in gratitude: to be seen, to be known, without revulsion. Then Alis' old strength pins her palm to the table.

"The Diasyrm?" Alis hisses. "The Theodisy War? Did you arrange it all?"

23. NIGH II [3667]

"No," Mara says, which is a lie told with truth.

"Do you understand what you've done? Have you reckoned the full cost?"

She has convinced tens of thousands of Awoken to abandon their immortality. She has deprived Distributary an infinite quantity of joy, companionship, labor, and discovery: all the works that might be accomplished by all the people who will join her in her mission to another world. When she lies awake at night, seized by anxiety, she tries to tally up the loss in her head. But it is too huge, and it becomes a formless thing which stalks her down the pathways of her bones like the creak of a gravity wave.

"Some infinities are larger than others," she tells her old captain. "I believe…we are here for a reason, and this is the way to fulfill that purpose."

"And how much would you sacrifice? Your mother? Your brother? Are the Awoken real to you at all?" Alis leans across her pinned hand, viper-fierce, striking. "Do you think my people were made to die for you?"

"Not for me. For our purpose. For our fate."

"For a home we abandoned. It's in the charter, Mara. The document on Shipspire that," and even Alis Li falls into a hush as she broaches one of the primal mysteries, her memory of creation, "that shaped the… the way I made this universe."

"You were the first," Mara acknowledges. "The first one here laid down the rules."

Alis Li releases her hand and collapses back into her chair. "Why are you here, Mara?"

To tell you the truth at last. "To ask you for that boon you owe me."

"At last." Alis sighs. "Well, I knew the day would come. I think I'll be glad to have this weight off my shoulders. You'll ask me to throw my support behind your mission, won't you? The First Queen says, go with Mara; awaken from this dream and go fight for your home. Is that it?"

"No," Mara says, with her heart in her throat, with trepidation bubbling in her gut. You cannot keep a secret buried like a vintage for so many centuries, and then unbottle it without any ceremony. "The boon I ask is your forgiveness."

Then she explains the truth. She tells Alis Li what she did: about the choice Alis Li would have made, if Mara had not made her own first. It's only an extension of what Alis has already deduced.

When she's finished, her ancient captain's jaw trembles. Her hands shake. A keen slips between her clamped teeth. The oldest woman in the world conjures up all the grief she has ever felt, and still it is not enough to match Mara's crime.

"You're the devil," Alis Li whispers. "I remember, in one of the old tongues, Mara means death…oh, that's too perfect. That's too much."

She laughs for a while. Mara closes her eyes and waits.

"You realize," Alis Li says, breathing hard, "that this is the worst thing ever done. Worse than stealing a few thousand people from heaven. Worse than that thing we fled, before we were Awoken—"

"Please," Mara begs. "Please don't say that."

Alis Li rises from her chair. "I'll support your fleet," she says. "I'll use every favor and connection I have to get your Hulls completed and through the gateway. And I will do it so that I can hasten your departure from this world. I will do it out of hate for you; I will do it so that every good and great thing we achieve here will ever after be denied to you, you snake. No forgiveness. Do you understand me? It is unforgivable. Go. Go!"

"I'd be very glad if you didn't tell my mother," Mara says.

Alis Li hurls the pitcher of blackberry tea over Mara, turns, and goes inside. Leaving her to trudge, wet and sticky but unbowed, back to her ship. She leaves her tea-stained parasol on the deck, but when she remembers it and looks back, it is already gone.

24. PALINGENESIS I [4355]

Mara thinks of the banyan trees that sprawl across the shallow silty lakes of a world she will never see again. The waveguides in her helmet detect the image and obey the encrypted command scheme she's rooted into every system in her fleet. She speaks into the flight directorate channel. "Flight. Sound off for final hold."

"FIDO. Go flight."

"Guidance. Go flight."

"INCO. Good constellation. Go flight."

"GEOD. Go flight."

"BIO. Go flight."

As her flight controllers confirm the state of their technical domains Mara looks out into space through the synthetic gaze of her sensorium. The Hulls gleam in the stark blue-white light of the star, each ship a silver seedpod braced by immense structural members and cocooned in reservoirs of spectrally adaptive smart fluid: theoretically enough to survive the horrible forces of transit through a singularity. Mara orders herself not to crane her neck. But she does it anyway, and gets a terrible cramp, as she searches the sky for Distributary.

There it is. The world of her rebirth, shining water-blue and beautiful, wrapped like a gyroscope in its twin rings. World of laughing corsairs, world of breathless forest hunts, world of mountains flickering with pale Cherenkov fire, world of sweet berry-stained lips and mathematical insight pure as a rhodium chime. She will never see it again.

Mara thinks of her mother. She doesn't want to but she does, and the memory blindfolds her and muzzles her and plugs her ears so she can hear nothing but Osana's voice on that final night. They're tipsy together, and the evening has wrapped around to morning: now they sit side by side, mother and daughter, watching the sun rise over the Chriseiad range from Osana's little ranch house on the tundra.

"I'm not coming with you," Osana says.

Mara has been so afraid of this answer for so long that she actually giggles. This can't be happening, of course, this is a nightmare, one of those stress dreams where your powers of persuasion and manipulation fail. "Sure, mom," she says, "you've got a ranch to run, after all. More?"

"No thank you." Osana squints into the dawn. Little age creases surround her eyes, illegible encryption, unbroken despite Mara's centuries of effort. The rising light draws a tear. "You'll have to send my goodbyes to Uldren. He's not speaking to me."

"What?" Mara gasps, as if this is the real shock, and not losing her mother forever. "Why?"

"Because I already told him I wasn't coming with you. I'm happy here."

"Mom," Mara says, with rising anger, "I'm happy here too. That's not the point—" A conversation which did not so much end as beat itself to an unsustainable emotional pulp, hours later. No catharsis. No closure.

Back in the present: "Weapons," Uldren calls. "Go flight."

"Go flight," Mara confirms. "The clock is counting. L minus five minutes." Directly off her Hull's bow, a sphere of ultradense mass waits for the moment of implosion and collapse. There will be only moments to transit the wormhole before it evaporates.

"Flight, Sensor," Sjur Eido calls. "I have anomalous starfield occlusions, bearing—"

"Intercept!" Mara shouts. "They're missiles!" It had to happen. Someone had to try to stop the departure, someone good and paladin-pure who believes they are saving tens of thousands of Awoken from madness and doom.

"Flight, FIDO. Do we abort?"

"Negative!" Mara snaps. "The countdown is go! Weapons, kill the inbounds!"

Sjur Eido grunts in dismay. "They're going to get through," she says. "Five or six, at least."

"Uldren." Mara opens their personal channel with the thought of his face. "Reassign your guns to protect the gateway."

"We'll lose Hulls, Mara—"

"I know. Do it." Mara opens the command interface for the gateway and sends the image of a bloody thorn. The countdown skips instantly to zero. "All ships, we are aborting directly to launch. Brace for acceleration!"

She issues the emergency launch order.

The Hull screams with thrust. Mara's suit floods with cushioning gel. She thinks of her mother's face, trying to fix it perfectly in her mind, and her sensorium tries, vainly, to open a channel to Osana. As the Hull plunges into the singularity, the last thing Mara sees is the mournful error message: No connection. No connection. No connection. Cannot connect to Osana.

25. PALINGENESIS II [2018]

Here in this time without time, pocketed by the ever-scattering cosm, touched as an assassin touches the gun in the secret fold. There is an eon within and I am going without. This is where we belong, interstitial, in that space between. This is where truth collapses supercritical.

There is a war and its name is existence. There are two ways to fight and one is the sword and one is the bomb.

By the sword I mean that way to fight which is tempered and solid. The way that is made from old things and which triumphs by the reduction to simplicity. This way is known to those who study the cosmos. Take any part of it at any time and you will see an edge and say 'This is a weapon.'

By the bomb I mean that way of being which is complex and schematic and which must attain a criticality to attack. The way that is made from new things and which triumphs by the arrangement of intricacy. This way is known to those who study themselves. Take any component of the bomb in isolation and you will say 'What is this, I cannot understand its purpose.' Yet there is in it the possibility of a fire.

Numberless are the spaces that surround the universe. Subordinate and superordinate are their relationships to the intrinsic world-that-is-only-itself. We pass now through analogy space which will reify what was once subject into object. That power which I held, which was agonist to a mother's rapprochement, will be realized and reified.

First is the awareness of my vector, which all who follow me held in their hearts.

Second is the desire to hear my speech, which all who follow me curled in their ears.

Third is the existence-at-the-fault, which is the inner tension that all who follow me still sense.

We are risen from man and fallen from heaven. We are made again in the fall. What was once us will not ever again be us. I am the uncrowned ever-Queen and my only diadem will be the event horizon of the universe which is my dominion. By falling I will rise.

There are an uncountable number of ways to be between zero and two.

26. PALINGENESIS III [3502]

The first hulk they colonized was a one-kilometer habitat tender, reactors still burning, gravity still steady at three-quarters of Earth's. Driven by an AI long ago reduced to basic subroutines, the tender had completed its final mission to wrangle an Oort-cloud comet down into the asteroid belt. When no orders came for the comet's disposition, it had set about gardening. The comet's surface was domed and soiled, and tethered mirrors kept taut by photon pressure focused starlight into a silvery radiance which fed the oxygen forest well enough. It would have been a marvel of greenery and ancient ice, but the surface had caught fire recently. Oxygen-fueled flame killed nearly everything except insects and rats. But Mara judged it would be a good fixer-upper, the rats the first intelligent life they had met since their return, the insects edible.

The Hulls had not survived the unpocketing as well as their passengers. The microsingularity wormhole, propped open by a precipitous spike of dark energy, pulled alloy and ceramic armor like taffy. Missiles mauled five of the Hulls. And worst of all, the passage through the nightmare limen between worlds had devastated onboard AI and logic systems.

It was time to abandon their cocoons. Uldren's survey located a reef of derelict spacecraft, apparently convoyed together for mutual aid in the Asteroid Belt. The Gensym Scribes who'd joined Mara on her journey were even now giddily cataloguing cultural markers and ancient records.

"We'll salvage the Hulls," Mara told Sjur Eido, "pull out the raw materials and the systems we can still use, and bring the biosystems of these hulks back online. Once we have reliable gravity, we can start having babies."

"We'll need weapons," Sjur said, cheerfully. "We don't have enough spare chemistry for firearms right now, and the maltech we brought with us would blow right through the hull. Also line-throwing tools. And devices for launching satellites off the surfaces of asteroids, hulks, et cetera. You know what I'm thinking?"

"I cannot say I can imagine," Mara said, sarcastically. She imagined the sight of Sjur Eido stringing her woman-tall bow, and passed the thought away like a card trick: dwelling on such pleasantries would not do. "Will it involve archery?"

"Big old compound bows with all sorts of tactical knickknacks." Sjur paced in delighted thought. "I'll be the first woman in the universe to place a comsat in heliocentric orbit with a longbow."

"You're absurd," Mara said, and, at Sjur's uninhibited grin of delight, at the thought of exploring and rebuilding this entire reef with her, even at the terrible flinch-thrill idea of sending Sjur into violence and danger, Mara felt a tingle of worrisome warmth and gladness.

"So," Sjur said, lunging into that moment of weakness to get what she wanted. "When will you tell everyone what's happened to Earth?"

At first they had thought Earth a ruin world. But there were signs otherwise. At least it had not turned into a machine-gnawed corpse like Mercury. "When Uldren's back from deploying his drones." She narrowed her eyes. "Sjur, can you hear what I'm thinking?"

"What, as in telepathically?" The Queen's bodyguard closed her eyes. "Everyone's been feeling spooky, but I'm not sure that extends to transmitting—Mara! Good grief!"

27. REVANCHE I [3889]

Uldren returned to the Reef during the Long Unquiet Night, when the Awoken people huddled in their beds and hammocks, gathered in ice caves and half-lit habitat cylinders, haunted by visions and portents. Faces appeared to them in the sublimating swirl of cometary ice: images and portraits in became impossible to distinguish from their real counterparts, so that all statues were shrouded, lest they appear to passers-by as corpses.

Something had changed in them after their return to the outer cosmos. A live-wire hum passed through the tendons in their hands, their jaws popped when they swallowed, and flashes of light like the impact of cosmic rays obscured their vision. It felt to Mara as if they had lowered their feet into an ocean of charge, and raised their hand to some invisible cable overhead: as if they were now again in contact with immense and opposing forces which had left an ancient mark.

"It feels like I've got scurvy," Sjur Eido snarled, having never had scurvy in her life. "As if all these old wounds in my soul are opening up again."

"People keep sending me notes," Mara said. Her sensorium had died in the transit, so the notes came to her through whispers and scraps of precious paper. "They say…I saw your face in my dream. I saw your eyes. I heard your voice."

"So it's not just me."

Uldren was the second person to bring her revelations on that day. First was Kelda Wadj, the Allteacher, one of Mara's most joyful recruits to the expedition: she was a master of pedagogy, able to mold any mind into a shape ready to learn, able to melt any fact into a fluid that could be poured. "I'm in from the Gensym labs," she said, "and they've learned something wonderful. We're all a bit magic now."

"Tell me more." Mara poured her a snifter of icy cometary water. "What does magic mean?"

"Some sort of weak acausality." Kelda lowered her flowerbulb build into a hammock of tangled plastic. "They've been firing encoded neutrino beams through volunteers, and it looks as if the resulting patterns of scatter depend on the cognitive and emotional state of the target. It's a very reliable detection, at least four sigma, but the effect size is terribly small."

Mara digested this with a shot of ancient ice, slushy against her tongue. "Acausality. You mean that whatever's happening—whatever influence we have on, say, neutrino beams—it's not accounted for by physics?"

"Not by any physics we know. At face it seems to violate some conservation laws, which would make Emmy Noether's head spin." Kelda remembers the names of her ancient physicist heroes even when she cannot tell which way is sunward.

"Secret physics." Mara thought of the Traveler and its works. "We've all felt it, haven't we? We know we're…" How to say 'trapped in the clinch between light and dark', she wondered, without quite so much portent? "We're in contact with certain numinous elements."

Kelda held out her cup for more water. "The question is, your Majesty— "

"Don't call me that. We're operating on a direct democracy here."

Kelda rolled her eyes. "The question is, do we continue to think of this as science? Do we teach it as physics? Causal closure says that everything which happens in a material system has a material cause. But if symbolic structures in the mind are triggering material effect…shouldn't we call that what it is?"

"Death had no dominion," Mara whispered.

"Pardon?"

"We're in Death's dominion now. We're all dying again. We were immortal on Distributary, weren't we? Some part of us was…attuned to the universe. And now that we're no longer receiving Distributary's signal, we're attuned to something new."

That was when the hatch slammed open and Uldren stumbled in, grinning ferociously, clutching a scummy fistful of cytogel to a slash across his neck.

"Aliens!" he rasped. "I found aliens, and one of them cut my throat!"

28. Revanche II

Mara calls a caucus of elected representatives in the Sacred Fire, one of the largest hulks in the reef of derelicts. The Fire was built to support habitat construction on 4 Vesta, where Mara hopes to one day anchor the entire flotilla and set down roots—but the hopeful, fearful faces before her make Mara afraid that it'll never happen. What if everyone runs off at the first hint of home? Having come so far, across worlds and eons, to see Earth again—how can she ask them to hold back now?

"We've found Humanity," she tells them. "We've found our ancestors."

The cheer of triumph and wonder thrills her to the marrow. Most of these Awoken are Distributary-born, raised on myths of Humanity and the Traveler. She has just opened the pages of their storybooks and conjured them to life.

"What remains of the Human species lives in a single settlement." She nods to Uldren, who snaps his fingers for footage. His ship's holographic perspective plunges through fluffy strata of clouds and mist, out into clear air. A lucid vista, a perfect instant: the white mountains, the city, and the enormous shattered sphere that hangs above it.

"Freeze," Uldren commands. "That is the Traveler."

As the crowd murmurs and thrills, Mara feels herself bridle. She doesn't like that thread of reverence. She doesn't like the Traveler looming there, almost but not quite completely dormant (like a dying heart ripped from its body and thrown into warm water, it ebbs and flutters if you look at it with the right sensors). If the Traveler had the power to protect anyone, wouldn't it protect more than one huddled settlement?

Esila, daughter of Sila, leaps up from the crowd, too small to make it on her own, but buoyed up by enthusiastic neighbors. "What are we waiting for?" she calls. "That's everything we came to find! They need us, and that's where we belong!"

Uldren and Mara trade glances. Uldren snaps his fingers, and the recording resumes.

Something moves in the treetops. The canopy roils and parts. A red-brown aircraft shaped like a fat, wingless, furiously angry dragonfly bursts from cover and climbs to intercept. Uldren's head-cued camera tracks the target, and Mara imagines his narrow grin as he waits for the other guy to make a move.

The dragonfly ship drops a brace of little needles, and they erupt into dirty orange flame and come arrowing after Uldren. Everyone in the caucus gets an earful of his grunts as he whips through a high-G turn and climbs away.

"Those are Fallen," Uldren says. "They're a species of interstellar scavengers and subsistence pirates. They've been here for a long time, and they've sacked most of the large settlements that survived the original fall of Humanity. There may be more Fallen than there are Humans left on Earth." He lifts his chin to bare the pale scar across his throat. "I landed and went looking for prisoners. I was ready when he pulled two knives on me, but it turned out he had an extra set of arms."

Nervous laughter.

"Worse," Mara adds, beckoning for panes of deep-space passive sensor data, "they're all over the solar system. We've detected flotillas of their interstellar ships around Jupiter and Venus. They don't go near Mars, but only because it's under occupation by another alien species. Mercury is—well, you can see for yourself." Gasps of horror at the clockwork cinder, all that remains of the legendary garden world. "We believe this may be the work of the Vex, a machine species listed in Shipspire's threat index."

Esila, famed historian, puts voice to the plea in the crowd. "So they need our help, don't they? We have to go to them! Our ships, our technology—we could make all the difference."

"No." Mara collapses the projected images between her hands. She stayed up late wrestling with this dilemma, which kept her from wrestling with Sjur. It was a choice she had to make alone. "We can't reveal our existence, lest the Fallen track us down. We need more information. Our focus must remain on securing this derelict reef, bootstrapping industry and a population, and scouting out the solar system."

"Mara, with all my respect, all my genuine gratitude for bringing us here," Esila sighs, "who died and made you Queen?"

Mara says nothing. But she thinks: Everyone, Esila. All of us died and made me Queen.

29. Revanche III

"It's bad," Sjur Eido says, confirming what Mara already knows, but nonetheless performing the valuable service of mopping away all the blood and tears and allowing Mara to glimpse the actual shape of the wound that divides her people. Not a literal wound (though she is, right now, tending to Uldren's scar, tweezing tiny fragments of Fallen metal out for analysis), but the rift in her Reef, the schism now re-schismatic, as if the quake that split the Distributary Awoken from Mara's people is now firing off aftershocks.

She should've known this would happen. She shouldn't have told them so much about Earth. "How bad?"

Sjur pokes Uldren in the hard gut, where a passing line of molten metal left a red burn. He's under anesthesia, but he snarls at her anyway. "As of the last caucus, I'd say thirty percent of the expedition wants to head for Earth. If you ask the 891," though there aren't 891 of them anymore, "it's more like eighty percent."

Mara swears and pulls a bloody line of solidified slag from her brother. "Unacceptable. We can't lose their skills." Or their genes: The Awoken have yet to adapt to the attrition of this harsh spaceborne world, and tentative mothers are still in the early stages of designing their babies. It's vital to maintain a diverse gene pool. "And the Fallen will vector them back to us."

"I know," Sjur says, heavily. "That's when I'm going to die."

The most horrible thing about the words is that they slap down on Mara's consciousness like face-up cards, like truth revealed. "Unacceptable!" she barks, and then both she and Sjur begin laughing, and then, at last, Mara shakes her head and growls. "You can't know that, Sjur. No one can know that."

"I do. I don't know how, but I do. I know it's going to be something I choose to do, and it's going to be incontrovertibly heroic. Which is enough for me."

"But if that's true—" Mara proposes, flinching away from the personal conversation they really ought to have, and all its attendant rawness, "—if you die when Fallen attack us, it means I won't stop these people from fleeing to Earth, and the Fallen are going to find us, and we're doomed." She is already building intricate models of how the universe might accommodate fate or doom and how she might go about destroying those things.

"Could be, I suppose." Sjur pulls a parchment-thin rag of dead flesh off Uldren's wound. "Look. I'm the Queen's bodyguard. I always expected I'd die violently."

"I'm not the Queen."

"Maybe that's your problem." She flicks Uldren in the chest, leaving a purple bruise, fading. "What is with you two, anyway? You never talk about him. You never seem to think about him at all. But he's dashing himself to pieces for you. How do you live as his favorite and only sister for so many centuries… and hardly even smile at him?"

Secrets, Mara thinks. You've got to have secrets from each other so there's room for him to fill in the gaps with his own happy illusions. Two ships joined together rigidly will tear each other apart if they try to move. But a loose tether leaves room to maneuver—and can be more quickly disengaged, if necessary.

That makes her think of Sjur's prophecy again. She sets the shrapnel down in the dissection dish, very gently. "You won't die. I won't allow it."

30. Revanche IV

Of all the disasters that might happen in space, riot is the worst. Breaches can be contained, fires can be starved, plague can be quarantined, radiation shielded, heat vented—but a riot has a will of its own: a chaotic ingenuity that corrodes any countermeasure.

Mara crawls through compartments choked with vaporized coolant. She keeps low and clutches the breather to her face. All she can think of is Kelda Wadj's last message and the data attached. "Mara. The paracausal effects are strongest around you. Whatever's happened to us, you are the locus. I cannot overstate how subtle and how important this discovery might be. Mara, when we use radioactive decay as a trigger for simulated bombs—bombs that could harm Awoken—the trigger atoms are a thousandfold less likely to decay near you. People are literally safer when you are around."

She has to get into the riot. She has to protect her people.

A horrible groan vibrates through the habitat structure, and then, with an apocalyptic shudder, something tears off the Reef. A ship. A ship is leaving. Mara has failed.

Mara drops onto her belly and pants into the mask. Then, cringing in anticipation of migraine, she activates the augment, the jury-rigged machine her eutechs produced for exactly this purpose by extracting Mara's ruined Distributary implants and reworking them. She's going to fire a command override to shut down that ship's systems—

—but then she realizes it's a salvaged Human vessel, deaf to her commands.

She gasps in frustration, sucking down cold bottled air. "Sjur."

"I'm here," her radio whispers. "Pinned down in the dockmaster's office. I shot a few in the shoulders, and they seem to have gotten the idea."

"Let them go. If one ship's away, there's no sense holding back the rest. Our position is compromised."

"Understood."

"Broadcast to everyone. I'm going to allow anyone who wants to leave the Reef to go. This their one and only chance." She rolls onto her back and stares up into the swirling vortices of coolant, seeing faces, futures, the lives she has just lost, the lives she might yet lose. She brought her people here to die in the sense that she brought them into mortality—but she never wanted it to happen quickly.

"They know, your Majesty," Sjur says. "They already know."

"What?"

"You told us. We heard your voice." Awe like gratitude in Sjur Eido's voice. "Mara, I heard you. You spoke to me."

31. Revanche V

Thus the riven Awoken were riven again, into Reefborn and Earthborn. Those who left went to scour the ruins for lost history and give some succor to their Human cousins who still clung to a hostile world. The Awoken came unto these Humans like nephilim, armed with lost weapons, forgotten industry and medicine. They were like omens of hope, for they were often taken to be starborn colonists returned to the hearth, which was not, after all, so far from truth. All who looked on them saw that the night sky contained more than lurking doom. They bred true with each other and sometimes hybridized with Humans, and in the course of centuries, many forgot the Distributary and even the Reef. However, there was always in their souls an itch, a vector pointing to a distant place in the Asteroid Belt, where their Queen still dwelt.

"They've made a difference already," Sjur told Mara not long after the first Awoken made planetfall on Earth. "They'll save so many lives just with the provision of medicine, pure water, and construction supplies that even if they all died by year's end, they would each yield ten or twenty Humans."

"I know," Mara said, with bitter pride. "Let the people remember them as saints and paladins, and tell no one how many more they might've saved if they had only kept the faith." For she knew the precious value of each Awoken life: She knew how many she would have to spend and mourned each soul wasted on a lesser purpose.

On the day the Fallen struck, Mara was proclaimed Queen. It happened swiftly, though after no little debate among the people, for everyone was afraid of a monarch who could speak to their thoughts. Yet they feared more to deny her power and sovereignty, for they had come between worlds in her name. To refuse her would be to refuse their choice.

"Awoken," she told them, "for the first time in my life, I hesitated to reach for power, and now one in three of you are gone. I cannot deny what the cosmos has made of me any longer. I am your one and rightful Queen."

She knew she had been a fool to pretend to be a peer to the others. What was true of her brother was true of all Awoken. They needed secrets to marvel at, secrets that rhymed with the deep enigma of their souls. They could not follow what they fully understood.

There would be a formal coronation later, in a place not yet built. Out of respect for that unhappened coronation, Mara did not at first wear a crown; and later she claimed as her diadem the ring of event horizon that surrounds the observable universe.

"My techeuns," she said, gathering Kelda Wadj and the other eutechs who'd remained, "will be given absolute authority to explore our new power, the Traveler's relics, and all associated domains. We are no longer in the realm of pure science. We require an order of mysteries and witches to tend to them."

Not an hour later, a Fallen Ketch threw off its stealth and began a deceleration burn toward 4 Vesta. The four-armed predators had traced one of the Earthward ships back through all its erratic course changes and to the Reef. They came in search of the source of these blue ape-kin.

A salvo of coherent-matter guns gutted the Ketch: blink-quick death for the mighty ship, ancient fury compressing matter into a relativistic pinhead. It was a waste of weapons that couldn't be recharged or reloaded, however, and the Baron in command had already scattered his skiffs like camouflaged seeds. The Fallen Raiders came down all over the Reef and cut their way inside. The Awoken, young to mortality, terrified of death, fled in fear.

Mara, Uldren, and Sjur Eido rallied as many as they could. Sjur fought in a powered combat shell, but Mara needed to be seen vulnerable, silver-haired and narrow-eyed, hurling herself at the enemy. She fought with pistol and dagger, and her brother moved like a wraith at her flank. Her people were ashamed of their timidity. No more were the Fallen scuttling alien predators: Now they were an indignity, an offense to regal privilege to be met with a snarl and a rifle shot. The Awoken saw their desperation: how the stump-limbed Dregs stumbled forward emaciated, how the Vandals cringed from battle as they peeled off wall panels, desperate for salvage to please their Captains.

Armored Sjur Eido met the Fallen Baron in zero-gravity combat above his spider tank and shot him dead, one adamant shaft through plate and throat. Ether hissed into vacuum. Sjur threw herself upon the spider tank that clung to the Sacred Fire's hull. Laughing in joy, she cut into the tank's barrel and threw a charge inside, knowing its next vengeful shot would be meant for the Sacred Fire's main habitat drum—and that she would die in the catastrophic misfire.

The tank fired. The charge detonated. Sjur Eido was thrown clear, utterly unharmed.

"That was where I should have died," she said, in wonder—and in her mind was the smiling face of her Queen.

32. Telic I

Mara made one more attempt, and only one, to call her scattered people home. She had hoped the assault would convince them they had a responsibility to the Reef, to come home and repair the damage they had caused. It went poorly, however, for though her tech witches were able to amplify her bond to her people through the augments Kelda had developed, she was only one voice in a maelstrom. Her Awoken had sensitive antennae, in the metaphysical sense, and could not hear her plea through the clamor. Also, the communications engineer kept forgetting to call Mara "Majesty" or "Queen."

"Good news," Uldren told her with the grim delight he always showed after a debacle he had survived. "Illyn and I went through the Fallen communications logs. Their Baron never transmitted our position to his Kell. He wanted the prize to himself. We remain secure."

"The Baron might have planted a time-delayed beacon," Mara warned him. "Never underestimate these beings. They've lived in the void longer than us."

"I already admire them," Uldren confessed. "They've lost so much. Some of them even ritually dismember themselves, Mara, to prove they have the strength to grow back the missing limbs. I tell you that even if we are doomed to dwindle and go extinct, those Fallen may outlive us."

Mara made a dry note in her log that her brother had at last discovered his true people.

For her part, Sjur Eido wandered about in a daze, filled with joy to be alive and grief that she no longer knew the day when she would die. "In you, all things are possible," she told Mara. "I live because of you." When Mara saw her string her mighty bow, the limbs coiled behind her leg and around her opposite arm, she was glad beyond telling that Sjur had survived.

In time, Mara appointed Paladins to oversee her new military, as Alis Li had done during the Theodicy War. She created talented starfarers as Corsairs, to scour the asteroid belt in utmost secrecy and to establish routes and caches that would support the covert motion of Awoken ships.

Most of all, she charged her brother with the mission that occupied her thoughts. "Brother," she said, "never again can I allow my people to be divided. We must offer them more than shielding ice and cold habitat cylinders and the warrens of Vesta. We must make a culture, a thread that binds us all in pride and wonder at the mystery of ourselves. Nowhere does culture flourish better than in a city."

"Gather in one place," Uldren warned her, "and you make yourself a target."

Mara had considered this, and found an answer. "Go forth and find me a power unknown to all the other powers of this world. Return it to me, and I shall make of it the cornerstone of my new city, where the Awoken shall dream of all they have been and all that is yet to come."

So Uldren went out voyaging among the worlds, swift as a blueshift ghost. In time, he returned to the Reef with a creature not larger than his hand, saying, "Behold, Sister, the lie that makes itself true. This is an Ahamkara."

33. Telic II

It was Mara alone who established a covenant with that young Ahamkara, which chose the use-name Riven, in honor of its host. It was Mara alone whose singular will and unity of purpose saved the Awoken from that which we now name the Anthem Anatheme. For there was in Mara very little division between Reality-As-Is and Reality-As-Desired; she was confident in her centuries of purpose and patient with the winding way by which the river of methods reaches the objective ocean. Blessed are those who in their absolute selfhood become selfless. Unappetizing are those who in their truest self-knowledge exclude the possibility of self-deceit.

"Mara," said Uldren Queensbrother, "why do you forbid me to speak to the Ahamkara?"

"This secret is mine alone," said Mara Queen. She knew that her brother had only widened the gap between He-As-Was (which is called NUME) and He-As-He-Would-Be (which is named CAUST). "Begone to the outer world, where I require thee."

This was when Sjur Eido, having spoken to Kelda Wadj and to Esila, at last came before her Queen. Kneeling, she said, "Your Majesty, Kelda Wadj says you are a god, for there is no difference between your desire and reality. Yet I know that you desire things before they ever become real. Esila says that you are keeping a secret from your brother that he must never know. I think the secret is thus: You are now a god because one day you will become a god, and a god is not temporal. Your brother is not a god because he will never become a god. Shall I worship you?"

"Sjur," Mara said, falling to her knees, clutching her beloved's face between shaking hands, "Sjur, on the day you worship me, you cannot love me anymore, for to worship is to yield all power, and I cannot love what has no power over me."

At this, the Ahamkara coiled around her neck, yawned, and showed its fangs: for there was a crevice between What Was and What Was Wanted.

"I see," Sjur Eido said. "Then to me you are not yet a god."

Although in time the knowledge of what Mara would become pushed them apart, it was a kind and happy push, as a friend might urge a beloved companion onward to a distant opportunity. And their days together were spent gladly.

34. Tyrannocide I

Mara's death began in this mark:

X

Later would come Eris Morn, Osiris, Toland, and all the other accessories of the majestic suicide. Later would come the Reef's tentative entanglements with Vex and Cabal, Fallen and Hive, and the fateful decision to intervene when the House of Wolves turned Earthward to conquer the Last Human City. Later, there would be stories here untold, the Ahamkara and the subcreation of the Dreaming City, the shatterstone fury of the Reef Wars, brother Uldren's journeys into that fell garden, and great sweeping plots whose beginnings and consequences have been entirely expunged for the sake of elegance—or, as of the root81, redacted for the sake of secrets yet untold.

Here is where the beginning began, at that moment when Mara bolted awake from the dream. Her circle of techeuns lay with her in the misty wintercold chamber, and they came back groggily, their augments stuttering with resync.

She had dreamt a thought of absolute simplicity and perfection, and the thought had become a tooth and bitten her. It had left a wound shaped like

X

Mara seized a pane of crystal paper, flashed it rigid and receptive with a touch, and wrote.

I DREAMT OF SWORD AND BOMB. I dreamt of the self-honing blade that has cut itself so fine, it pierces the world and thus becomes the world. It is self-honing because it constantly whets itself against itself. I dreamt of Death bearing this blade, or of something so closely allied with Death as to be its synonym, so that to separate them would require a knife sharper than sharpness. Death raised up that blade and said "I cut all and all I cut. Aiat."

Then Death cut the bomb, and the bomb was broken and could not fire. I was in the bomb. I knew that Death was the cut-verb, and that its only verb was to cut.

SHAPES AND GLIDERS. I dreamt of existence as a game of cellular automata. In this metaphor, there were only two things: shapes in the game world and the rules of the game world. The rules were the rules of Life and Death. I understood that the sword was the desire to escape existence as a shape in the game and to become the rule that made the shapes. This rule said only "live" or "die"—it had no other outputs. It could not keep secrets. Against it was the desire to become a shape so complex that it could within itself play other games.

WHAT WILL SOON BE. I dreamt that the Sword that was Death and Rule sought out complexity and cut it to reveal the simplicity within. I knew that soon we would be cut for we were complex and full of secrets. I knew that it was coming. I knew that the stroke would fall and that I had to stop it.

HOW CAN A BOMB MAKE USE OF A SWORD?

HOW CAN THE RULE THAT SEPARATES LIFE FROM DEATH BE KILLED?

"I must go to the Dreaming City and use the oracle engine," Mara told her techeuns. "Prepare my ship."

35. Tyrannocide II

Ten times and once more Mara asked the oracle engine to show her the sword that was death and the way it would appear. Ten times and once more the oracle engine showed Mara an image of her family.

First it showed her Sjur Eido, laughing and bright with strength, who would recede and later return.

Then it showed her Uldren, her brother, who explored the ruins of the fallen worlds and sought out challenges to test himself.

Then it showed Mara her own face and lingered on the secret brightness of her eyes.

Last of all, leaving Mara imperious with disdain toward her own feelings, curtly aloof toward all who asked her what troubled her, it showed her Osana, who had remained behind.

Mara dwelt on this puzzle. A mother who had remained behind; a sister with secrets; a brother who hunted and explored; a woman who was plain and fierce. She understood then that the answer to her question lay within herself and that to defeat what was coming, she would need a perfect understanding of herself. Isolation would be her watchword, for an isolated system is easiest of all to understand.

First of all, Mara went into the gardens and planted a flower for her mother, who she thought must still live: though she might by now have forgotten her first daughter and her first son.

"Mother," she said, "I asked to be your sister rather than your daughter, and so I denied you the chance to tell me your secret, the mothertruth that is mapped in the negative space defined by the lies mothers tell their daughters. Well, here are my secrets. I love you. I have always loved you. Without you, I could never have been anything at all."

Then she went to speak to her brother—but Uldren was away on Mars, and she found only his empty chambers, the half-sharpened knives and racks of pistols. She knelt in grief and touched her hand to the floor where his pacing boots had scuffed the asteroid stone smooth. This was the shape of their siblinghood now. The pursuit of absences.

Last of all Mara went to Sjur Eido. Sjur was making a list of incredibly stupid and fatal tasks to post on a Guardian bounty board. "I want to tell you the truth," Mara said. "Ask me a question."

"If you take any positive integer and halve it if it's even, but triple it and add one if it's odd, and you repeat this process forever, will you always, eventually, reach one?" Sjur Eido demanded.

"Sjur, my faithful Wrath," Mara said, "please take my openness seriously. Though I'm sure Illyn could answer your math problem."

"Okay." Sjur looked at her curiously. "Then here's my question. What's gotten into you? Why are you acting like this?"

"Can we walk?" Mara asked her.

36. Tyrannocide III

Mara and Sjur Eido go out into space and kick off the hull, wearing Corsair skin-pressure suits and slim tethers. The stars circle them like hard-focus candles, like the diadems of a trillion dancers. Sjur Eido pulls herself close and touches helmets with Mara. "We're alone. What's happened, Mara? You've always been, ah…"

"Private?" Mara suggests.

"Mysterious and reclusive, I was going to say."

"A sword can be part of a bomb if the swordstrike is the detonation mechanism," Mara says. "It's impossible for a cellular automata game to change its own rules, but it is possible to create subgames with their own rules, and for those subgames to yield advantage in the master game."

"That's cool," Sjur says. "You know, when you talk like that, what you're actually saying is, 'I don't want anyone to understand me, but I want them to understand they don't understand me.'"

"Yeah," Mara admits, and then, hoarsely, she makes herself say, "Sjur, I have this secret, this thing I did, and I don't know if anyone can know it without hating me forever."

"I had a secret too," Sjur reminds her. "The thing I did…"

"It's nothing compared to mine. Nothing at all."

"Having had some long experience hating you, and then having given it up, I think it would be hard for me to go back." Sjur's strong hand settles at the small of Mara's back. They twirl on upward, rotating around a point between them, their thousand-kilometer tethers slowly unfurling. "Do you want to tell me?"

"No," Mara says. "But I think I have to."

"Okay. Your Majesty, what did you do that made Alis Li throw blackberry tea in your face?"

"I was first," Mara says. And she explains the missing half, the first half of the sentence:

I made the rules and initial conditions that deceived her into believing she herself had decided

It ends like that, where the rest picks up.

Sjur Eido looks at her in expressionless silence. Sjur Eido's hands stroke the seam between Mara's skinsuit and the glassy petals of her helmet. Long ago, this woman betrayed her oath and went to serve the Diasyrm, a woman who cried out in anguish at the curse of physicality and the possibility of suffering. Long ago, this woman threw away her whole life to punish the highest crime she could imagine: the denial of transcendent divinity to those who might have claimed it.

"You're the devil," Sjur says. "You're the lone power who made death. You allowed the possibility of evil. You might be responsible for more preventable suffering than anything that has ever existed."

Mara cannot shake her head or even nod.

"Well," Sjur says, "if you hadn't, none of us would be here. I guess I don't see what else you could've done, if you cared about those we left behind. If you wanted us to be able to go back and help in the fight." She leans forward and very gently kisses the inside of her helmet, where it meets Mara's: in her mind, in that place that is bound to all other Awoken, Mara feels the touch of gentle lips.

Sjur looks suddenly sly. "You know, Mara, I don't think you could've confessed anything, anything at all, unless it were a way of keeping a deeper secret. What's really going on?"

"There are many ways to godhood," Mara tells her. The belt of Orion glitters on her helmet like a three-star rating left by some Hive entity Sjur once killed. "One way is to kill all that is killable, so all that remains must be immortal. Another is the road I have walked, mostly by accident. One of these ways is closer to the sword, and one is closer to the bomb. If the bomb can defeat the sword by the standard of the sword, then the bomb has claim to primacy."

"Never mind," Sjur sighs. "Seen anything cool on Crow surveillance lately?"

37. Tyrannocide IV

Later. Much later. It is the night before the day of screams. Mara meditates cross-legged in a cradle of null gravity. Variks has told her more than once how the Fallen speak of the Awoken as sterile, unable to regrow their flesh, cursed to bear their scars forever. Also how they think of the Awoken as self-twinned, coexisting with their own shadows. Didn't ancient Inanna, queen of heaven, descend into the underworld to confront her shadow twin, sister Ereshkigal?

Inanna was judged full of hubris and executed.

You cannot defeat a thing that is synonymous with death except on its own territory. You cannot fear and flee from death. You must face it. Death is a sword, and a sword is like a crossing-point, like a bridge—and a bridge may be walked two ways.

The plan exists in her mind alone, although beloved Eris has by necessity learned most of it. The Techeuns do not know the whole plan, although they will position the Harbingers upon the threshold. Even sweet capable Petra does not know the whole plan.

So many she will leave behind.

Uldren knows nothing of the whole plan. He has kept more and more to himself, building up secrets and schemes—all, Mara knows (and pities), because he needs Mara and thinks he can get her attention by keeping secrets from her.

Secrets are her virtue and the virtue of her nemesis. The being whose existence she deduced from the analogy-of-family the Oracle Engine showed her.

Mara will begin the end of that Queen's brother today. She knows what that means for the fate of her own. An eye for an eye. She must think now of the fate of entire cosmos—and of her tender, half-assembled answer to the cold sword logic of the Hive. She must not grieve. She must not fear.

Was Inanna afraid when she descended? Mara's not going to be outclassed by some ancient fable. After all, Mara's name is death. But there is one thing she admires most about Inanna over all the other myths of katabasis.

Inanna went to conquer.

38. Tyrannocide V

She closes her eyes. Oryx's throne world smashes through her fleet, the bubble of everted screamspace pulverizing rock, metal, and flesh as mere matter surrenders to the will-made-fact of the Taken King. Somewhere, Uldren roars defiance. This is the moment of absolute sacrifice, the incarnation of Awoken doom: to give up their lives in defense of the world they once abandoned. The sense of their great dying rips at Mara like a sob.

She feels her techeuns preparing emergency selfgates. Shuro Chi reaches out to her—a wordless, urgent need for Mara to live—and it takes all the cold impassive remove of Mara's millennia to turn that hand away.

The shockwave strikes.

Mara dies.

In one way, she is vaporized with her Ketch, the bonds between the very particles of her body questioned by the harrowing logic of Oryx's weapon and found inessential. The mechanism of devastation is spontaneous fission. The author of the devastation is laughing in joy.

In another way, a more true and symbolic way, she is impaled on Oryx's blade. She has thrown all her might at him, and he has answered. He has snuffed her fledgling divinity and her meager claim to royalty, he has exposed Mara to the raw and caustic hostility of his High War. She has been defeated by the sword logic.

She dances down the blade and steps into his throne world. The Harbingers give her the gate and she takes the step. She is dead, consumed by Oryx: She is dead in his will, his Ascendant Realm. There was no other way inside except this true way.

Inanna at least gave her people some warning; she told her minister to have her worshippers lament, drum, pray, and lacerate their buttocks. Inanna told her minister to beg the gods to save her. Mara has not. Instead, she has enlisted Eris and several million mad dancing Guardians to go knock off the god who killed her. It is, on that level, a very simple bank heist: Get yourself taken into the treasury as treasure, and when the owner dies, break back out with his stuff.

But even Inanna had to send everyone away before she passed through the last door.

Mara thinks of everyone she has ever known, all the people she has lost, back even to *Yang Liwei* and that ray of Light in deepest Darkness. She is there again, on the tether, falling into the mystery. Her brother is crying out after her, trying to follow, and she cannot look back.

She has been thinking of a logic of her own, of secrets and hidden designs. The universe has not grown simpler in its age. Wherever life can begin, it has begun, and even in some places where sensible folk expect it should not. The great tendency has been toward intricacy, toward sophistication, toward deep thought and richer ways of being. A sword is everywhere edged, but the pieces of a bomb do not look at all like weapons until they are assembled.

Oryx's throne world tries to tear her body and psyche into a quintillion screaming pieces, but Mara has survived the inchoate primordial chaos before space and time. She has retained her selfhood through far worse than this—and she has patience for eons. Eris will succeed. The Guardians will play their part. When the power in this world is free for the taking, Mara will take it, not as the victor taking spoils, but as a scavenger takes a prize component for her masterwork.

When a pawn reaches the far side of the chessboard, it may be promoted to a queen. And what hatches when you promote a queen? What new board does she claim her place on?

Mara knows.

She settles in for the long wait, entirely alone, almost at peace with it.

NARRATIVE IN:

The player followed the whispers of Cayde-6 into the Dreaming City, a surreal shrine world that the Awoken claim to own.

EXT. SHORES OF .THE DREAMING CITY - DAWN

Silver waves TOSS the GUARDIAN onto a spit of wet sand. They lay there, half-drowned, GHOST clutched in their fist.

Nearby, an ancient SALT-CRUSTED HIVE WARSHIP hangs suspended inexplicably in the air, blasted into dozens of plasma- charred pieces.

The shoreline wraps around a rocky coast. An elegant AMETHYST TOWER juts defiantly from the cliffside, a feat of gravity- defying engineering. EDDIES OF MIST obscure the horizon, but the ALIEN SKY of this place is undeniable: above, FOREIGN MOONS orbit the accretion disc of a BLACK HOLE.

Where are we...?

THE GUARDIAN STANDS, allowing GHOST to float out of their hand. They give their gun a quick once-over.

> MARA SOV (O.S.)
> (grieving)
> Hundreds of my subjects died for this plan.

THE GUARDIAN SNAPS TO ATTENTION, readying their gun. Just up the beach, partially obscured by mist--

MARA SOV sits, hunched, KNEELING in the sand.

> MARA SOV
>
> "Subjects." Hmph. My friends. My family...

Drawing closer, we see MARA is cradling ULDREN'S BODY in her lap, a mirror of the Guardian cradling Cayde's body.

In death, ULDREN looks frail.

MARA blazes with bitter grief. She loved her brother. She loved her people, too.

> MARA SOV
>
> Hundreds of the Awoken are dead because of me. Hundreds, gone forever, or resurrected as a war drone for your Traveler. And you don't even realize we've done it all to help save humanity.
> (beat)
> You think we're *enemies*.

MARA GLARES up at the Guardian, unflinching. She's faced far worse than this since we last saw her. She's conquered death.

So has the Guardian. Still, THEY LOWER THEIR GUN

> THE GUARDIAN
>
> I saw something that looked like you. Some kind of illusion.

MARA SOFTENS. She looks down at Uldren.

> MARA SOV
>
> I know.

SHE STROKES HIS HAIR.

> **MARA SOV (CONT'D)**
> This --
> > (beat; a difficult truth)
>
> -- was not part of the plan...
> > (forgetting her audience)
>
> It's my fault he went into the Garden... My fault he killed your friend...

> **GHOST (O.S.)**
> > (with compassion)
>
> That's not true.

MARA LOOKS UP. She SHIFTS ULDREN TO THE SAND, sister-tender, then rises, composed and imperious. The Queen of the Awoken.

> **MARA SOV**
> I will set this right.

She STEPS CLOSER to the Guardian, chin tipped upward.

> **MARA SOV**
> And you, the Chosen Dead, will help me.

The Guardian glances at GHOST, then NODS.

None of them notice the SHADOWY APPARITION OF CAYDE-6, watching from the clifftops...

NARRATIVE OUT:

The player will learn about the monster that lured them into the Dreaming City and drove Uldren to madness.

TO EVERYONE WHO INSPIRED US, WHO SHARED OUR DREAM,
AND WHO WALKED WITH US ON THIS INCREDIBLE JOURNEY
—TO EVERY MEMBER OF THIS BRILLIANT COMMUNITY—
THANK YOU FOR BEING THE MOST IMPORTANT CHARACTERS
IN THE WORLDS WE BUILD.

DESTINY GRIMOIRE ANTHOLOGY, VOLUME IV: THE ROYAL WILL

Based and built on the inspiring work of the talented individuals at Bungie—too numerous to note—who have each contributed to these words in their own unique and important ways.

Bungie

Contributing Writers

Bungie Cinematic Team:
xvi, 37

Clay Carmouche:
39

Seth Dickinson:
x-xi, 4-7, 9, 10, 15, 25, 27, 28, 40, 43-46, 48-54, 56-66, 70

Jason Jones:
6

Ted Kosmatka:
55

Lucy Prebble:
3, 13, 17, 21

Eric Raab:
1, 6, 9, 10, 19, 20, 34

Robert Reed:
16

Jill Scharr:
11, 14, 29, 31, 32, 35, 41, 67

Z Schleif:
1, 35, 71, 152-154

Jon To:
47

Michael Zenke:
40, 68

Jill Scharr with Z Schleif:
35

Seth Dickinson with Z Schleif:
The Marasenna 73-147

Bungie

Editor, Art Direction, and Design:
Lorraine McLees

Art Direction and Cover Design:
Garrett Morlan

Illustrations:
Richard Anderson

Additional art:
Jesse van Dijk
Jaime Jones
Kekai Kotaki

Graphic Design:
Spencer Shores
Tim Hernandez

Destiny Universe Leadership
Mark Noseworthy
Luke Smith

Destiny 2 Narrative Director
Adam Grantham

Franchise Art Direction:
Michael Zak

Grimoire Curator and Editor:
Eric Raab

Additional Curation/Editorial:
Christine Feraday

Layout:
Dan Caparo

Production:
Chris Hausermann

Copy Editor:
Laura Scott

Legal:
Bungie Legal Team

Director, Consumer Products:
Katie Lennox

Blizzard Entertainment

Production:
Anna Wan
Derek Rosenberg

Director, Consumer Products Publishing:
Byron Parnell

www.bungie.net

© 2021 Bungie, Inc. All rights reserved.
Destiny, the Destiny logo, Bungie and
the Bungie logo are among the
registered trademarks of Bungie, Inc.

Published by Blizzard Entertainment, Inc.,
Irvine, California, in 2021.

No part of this book may be reproduced
in any form without permission from the publisher.

Library of Congress Cataloging-in-Publication Data available.

ISBN: 978-1-950366-57-6

10 9 8 7 6 5 4 3 2 1

Manufactured in China